Dear Napoleon,
I Know You're
Dead, But ...

OTHER YEARLING BOOKS YOU WILL ENJOY:

AWFULLY SHORT FOR THE FOURTH GRADE, *Elvira Woodruff*
THE SUMMER I SHRANK MY GRANDMOTHER, *Elvira Woodruff*
THE DISAPPEARING BIKE SHOP, *Elvira Woodruff*
EARTH TO MATTHEW, *Paula Danziger*
EVERYONE ELSE'S PARENTS SAID YES, *Paula Danziger*
MAKE LIKE A TREE AND LEAVE, *Paula Danziger*
THE CAT ATE MY GYMSUIT, *Paula Danziger*
NOT FOR A BILLION GAZILLION DOLLARS, *Paula Danziger*
GRUEL AND UNUSUAL PUNISHMENT, *Jim Arter*
COACH AMOS, *Gary Paulsen*

YEARLING BOOKS/YOUNG YEARLINGS/YEARLING CLASSICS are designed especially to entertain and enlighten young people. Patricia Reilly Giff, consultant to this series, received her bachelor's degree from Marymount College and a master's degree in history from St. John's University. She holds a Professional Diploma in Reading and a Doctorate of Humane Letters from Hofstra University. She was a teacher and reading consultant for many years, and is the author of numerous books for young readers.

For a complete listing of all Yearling titles,
write to Dell Readers Service,
P.O. Box 1045,
South Holland, IL 60473.

Dear Napoleon, I Know You're Dead, But ...

Elvira Woodruff

drawings by Noah and Jess Woodruff

A Yearling Book

For the wittiest one on Vanderveer Road,
Frank G., of course
E.W.
N.W.
J.W.

Published by
Bantam Doubleday Dell Books for Young Readers
a division of
Bantam Doubleday Dell Publishing Group, Inc.
1540 Broadway
New York, New York 10036

ISBN: 0-440-40907-1

Reprinted by arrangement with Holiday House, Inc.

Printed in the United States of America

October 1994

10 9 8 7 6 5 4 3 2 1

Chapter 1

Martin Bellucci
% Midbury Elementary School
Midbury, New Hampshire 03301

Dear Napoleon,

I know you're dead, but there aren't any famous people alive who I want to write to. You see, our teacher, Miss Gerbino, gave our fourth-grade class this assignment. We have to write a letter to a famous person. She said that it would be fun to ask them about their life and see if they answered our letters. A lot of kids are writing to movie stars or baseball players, and even though I like some of them, I don't really have anything I want to ask them.

I have a lot of questions to ask you, though. I guess it all started with my gramps. He used to live with us, and he told me all about you. My gramps and I used to work in the garage together. We made a special birdhouse for bluebirds. Gramps got sick before we could hang the house up, though. So I'm keeping it in my room until he's better.

My gramps knows a lot about history, more than anyone I know. He knew all the battles you fought in and how you ended up in exile on an island.

I was wondering what the island was like. Were you lonely there? Were there lots of sharks swimming around the island, so that you couldn't swim away? Did you miss your army? And did you know that they named a dessert after you? I wish you could write back.

Your friend,
Martin Bellucci

P.S. Everyone calls me Marty, except my gramps. He calls me Mars Bars.

P.P.S. I have some army men that I pretend are you and your soldiers.

Miss Gerbino shook her head as she stood over Marty's desk. "Marty, I'm afraid you don't understand," she said. "We're writing to famous people who are alive, so they can write back to us. Napoleon has been dead for a long time."

Marty frowned. "I know. But you said to choose someone who we really wanted to write to, and I wanted to write to Napoleon."

"But Marty, Napoleon won't be able to answer your letter," Miss Gerbino pointed out. "Wouldn't it be better to write to someone who could write back?"

Marty's shoulders slumped as he sank down in his seat.

"Why don't you see if you can think of someone else?" Miss Gerbino said gently.

Marty watched as she stopped at his friend Russell's desk. Russell McGrath was pencil thin and had a crop of carroty red hair. Marty knew that Russell was probably writing to Ken Griffey, Jr., the baseball player. Russell loved baseball and was sure Ken Griffey, Jr., would be in the Baseball Hall of Fame one day. Russell would probably get a letter back, because his famous person was alive, and his face on Russell's baseball card looked especially friendly. He might even send Russell a signed ball.

Marty watched as Miss Gerbino smiled and moved on to Jessica Hollander's desk. Marty could guess who Jessica was writing to. Everyone in the class knew that Jessica was in love with ballet. She was always dancing around the room, twirling up to the chalkboard or doing little jumps down the hall. Once she had even brought in her hard-toe ballet shoes to show Miss Gerbino. Jessica's favorite dancer was Andrea Markoff. She had taped pictures of her to her notebook and her lunchbox. She had probably written to Andrea Markoff, and the ballet star would probably send her a picture of herself dancing.

Miss Gerbino nodded as she read Jessica's letter. Marty looked down at his own letter. A letter to a dead person. He carefully folded it and stuffed it into his back pocket. Who else could I write to? Who? he wondered, as he closed his eyes to think. Marty always closed his eyes tight when he had to do some serious thinking. He liked the way everything went black, except for little sparks of light. It reminded him of the sky at night, with stars. A starry night. He opened his eyes and grinned. Then Marty picked up his pencil and began to write,

Dear Vincent van Gogh,
  I know you're dead, but . . .

Chapter 2

Martin Bellucci
% Midbury Elementary School
Midbury, New Hampshire 03301

Dear Vincent van Gogh,
  I know you're dead, but I really wanted to write to you anyway. My gramps used to have two of your pictures hanging in his bedroom. Gramps let me pick one to keep before he left for the nursing home. It was hard to choose. I really liked the yellowy orange sunflowers, because yellow is my favorite color. I finally picked Starry Night, though, because it reminded me of the night I camped out in our backyard. Gramps helped me build a fire, and we roasted marshmallows. Later I slept in my tent, but Gramps slept in the house. We

laughed a lot that night. It was before he got sick. The stars were shining so brightly that Gramps said you must be smiling somewhere. He told me all about you, how you loved the sky and the trees, and how you never had enough money for paints and no one wanted to buy your pictures, but you kept on painting anyway. Gramps said that in your paintings you were very happy, but in your life you were very sad.

I was wondering, what made you so sad? The day Gramps left for the nursing home, I think I felt as sad as you. I helped my mom pack his things. When she took the sunflower picture off the wall and put it in the suitcase, we both started to cry. She took it out of the suitcase and told me to carry it instead. Somehow it just seemed wrong to shut such happy flowers away in a suitcase.

I know you can't write back, but I wish you could.

Your friend,
Martin "Mars Bars" Bellucci

"A dead person? Why would you want to write a letter to a dead person?" Russell asked while he and Marty ate lunch. Everyone at the table was talking about their letters.

"There's no one alive that I want to write to," Marty said. He bent his head of wavy brown hair over his open lunchbox. When he finally looked up, he rolled his dark eyes to the ceiling. "Not again," he moaned. "If I eat one more turkey sandwich, I'm going to throw up."

"Or start to gobble." Russell laughed. "Why does your mom make you so many turkey sandwiches?"

"I don't know," Marty said. "When Gramps was living with us, he would make my lunch, and I got good stuff like cream cheese and raisin bread or salami." Marty stared down at his sandwich. "I wonder if it would taste better with the turkey on the outside and the bread on the inside." He pulled the two slices of turkey out of the sandwich. He placed them along with the lettuce on the outside of the bread.

Russell shook his head. "You're the only person I know who would think of turning his sandwich inside out to make it taste better, but I guess that figures, because it's about as weird as writing a letter to a dead person. So, how does it taste?"

"Much better." Marty closed his eyes and threw his head back dramatically. "It doesn't even taste that much like turkey anymore. You should try it."

Russell looked down at his ham and cheese sandwich. "But what if the lunch monitor sees us? Do you remember that lecture Mr. Bullner gave us all last week, the one about not playing with our food?"

"But this isn't playing, this is rearranging," Marty pointed out. "Oh, go ahead, Russ," he coaxed. "Sometimes you just have to do stuff that pops into your head, without worrying about it."

"I am kind of tired of ham and cheese the same old way," Russell mumbled, taking the slices of ham and cheese out of his sandwich and placing them on the outside of his bread. "Um, you're right." He grinned. "It is much better this way."

Marty looked around the table and his dark

eyes lit up. "I have a great idea," he whispered. "Today is hoagie day, so even the kids
who bought their lunch have sandwiches. Let's
see how many kids we can get to turn their
sandwiches inside out."

Russell moaned. "Oh no, not another great
idea," he said. Last week, Marty had suggested they keep their mouths open during
social studies. Marty said that maybe if they
kept their mouths open long enough, they
could get into *The Guinness Book of World
Records*. Russell had been sitting with his
mouth open for four and a half minutes when
Justin Massey walked by and dropped his
eraser onto Russell's tongue. It was not a pleas-
ant experience, since Justin usually carried his
eraser in his sneaker. The eraser had an awful
foot-in-the-mouth taste.

"Come on," Marty said. "Wouldn't it be
neat to see if we could get everybody at the
whole table to turn their sandwiches inside
out? And then maybe another table." His voice
rose with excitement. "And then another, and
then maybe the whole lunchroom. Just think
of it, Russ, the whole lunchroom! I bet that

would get us in *The Guinness Book of World Records.*"

Russell giggled. "It does sound like a pretty good idea," he whispered. "Do you really think we could do it?"

"Just watch," Marty said confidently. He looked over at Adam Gartner and commented on what a boring-looking sandwich he had. It didn't take Marty more than a minute to convince Adam to try turning his bologna sandwich inside out. Soon the entire table was reversing their sandwiches, all except Denise Donnalson, who thought the idea was "too gross." Marty jumped up from his seat.

"Where are you going?" Russell wanted to know.

"I'm going to get us in *The Guinness Book of World Records,*" Marty said. He walked over to the lunch line, pretending to need a straw. On his way, he convinced Danny Kline that roast beef and mustard would taste much better on the outside of the bread. Danny then turned to Eli Meiser, and before long a second table was taking part in Marty's latest craze. Russell, meanwhile, went up to the line and on the way back stopped at a table of second graders. They were more eager to try "outsiding," especially after a big fourth grader told them how cool it was.

"I can't believe you finally had a great idea that really worked," Russell whispered, sitting down at their table. Marty looked around the lunchroom and grinned. Kids at all the tables were busy turning their sandwiches inside out.

"I can't believe that I didn't think of it sooner," Marty said. "This will definitely get us into *The Guinness Book of*—" But before he could finish his sentence, there was a scream at table number five. Marty and Russell looked up to see little Willy Horvath, a first grader, trying to turn his tuna fish sandwich inside out. Globs of tuna fish were falling everywhere. Annie Franneli, who was sitting beside him, was crying that he had ruined her chocolate cupcake with a glob of tuna fish. Another glob had fallen into Stevie Gallia's thermos of milk.

At another table, Megan Bailor had already turned her jelly and peanut butter around and was trying to wipe off the jelly that had spilled onto Sara Kessler's white blouse. It wasn't long before the entire lunchroom erupted into complete chaos.

Suddenly Mr. Bullner (or the Bull, as some kids called him behind his back) appeared. Mr. Bullner, the gym teacher, had lunch duty on Friday. This was the worst day for teachers in the lunchroom. Everyone was usually noisier at the end of the week. Miss Pessin, the principal, knew that it would take a powerful show of force to keep order in a Friday lunchroom, a force that could strike terror into even the rowdiest luncher, so she picked Mr. Bullner to do lunch duty that day. He was a huge barrel-chested man, with a thick red neck and tiny green eyes. What little hair he had shot out of his head in short, angry blond spikes. His arms and legs were thick with bulging muscles. Marty imagined that if you stared at Mr. Bullner long enough, you could probably watch his muscles grow.

Mr. Bullner didn't need to flex any muscles to instill fear into the lunchroom. He only needed to blow his big silver whistle. He wore it around his neck on a thin black cord. When Mr. Bullner wanted silence, he blew the whis-

tle once. When he was angry, he blew it twice.
And when things got really bad, he blew it
three times.

Marty and Russell slumped in their seats.
They winced as they heard Mr. Bullner blow
his whistle once, twice, and then a third time!
A deathly silence fell over the lunchroom, followed by the slight rustling of paper as a few
trembling lunchers clutched their brown bags
in terror.

Mr. Bullner's strained voice cut through the
silence in short, stabbing jabs. "I want the person or persons responsible for starting all this,
and I want them now!"

Chapter 3

"*The Guinness Book of World Records*, yeah, right," Russell whispered sarcastically, as he and Marty sat alone in the reading room. They had been ordered there by Mr. Bullner, where they were to write the sentence *I will never disrupt the lunchroom again* one hundred times.

"One hundred times! Do you know how long it will take us to write this sentence one hundred times?" Russell groaned.

"Mr. Bullner must have a thing for the number one hundred," Marty said, looking up from his paper. "The last time he gave us a punishment, for talking those first graders into eating all that Play-Doh, he had us write one hundred sentences too." Marty sighed wearily as he realized he was only on sentence number fourteen. He gripped his pencil tighter and began number fifteen.

"I still think it was a great idea," he mumbled. "We could have gotten into *The Gui—*"

"The only thing your great ideas ever get us into is trouble," Russell interrupted.

Both boys grew quiet as they listened to the voices of their classmates laughing and shouting on the playground.

"The Bull said that we can't have recess until we finish all one hundred sentences. That could take us weeks." Russell groaned again.

"My hand is getting numb," Marty said. "Maybe we could finish the rest with our feet."

"Our feet?"

"Yeah, my gramps once told me about a man who could write with his toes. Gramps said there are all kinds of ways to do things, and people shouldn't get stuck doing everything the same way."

"I think it would be really hard to write with your feet," said Russell.

"I know," Marty agreed. "But Gramps said that if you concentrated, you could do it. He said that a person should cultivate his powers of concentration. If our hands are getting numb, we can concentrate and use our feet. Why don't we try it?"

"I think your brain is getting numb," Russell sighed. "Just keep your sneakers on, will you? I don't know where you get these ideas anyway. Aren't we in enough trouble? Writing with our toes—that's all we need. It's as goofy as writing to dead people." He looked over at Marty, who was staring down at his sneaker.

"Why don't you write to a ballplayer like Will Clark or Matt Williams?" Russell suggested. "You'd probably get a letter back from them. My dad is taking me to see the San Francisco Giants play when they come to New York. Maybe you could come with us and see Will Clark in person."

Marty shook his head and returned to sentence number fifteen. "Naw, I don't think so." Both boys fell silent as they continued to write.

Marty thought about going to see the Giants play. He didn't really like baseball all that much, not the way the McGraths did. Russ and his father lived and breathed baseball.

They watched all the games on TV and checked all the scores in the newspapers. Mr. McGrath had even given Russell what was left of his old boyhood baseball card collection. There were only six cards, compared to the hundreds Russ had collected, but Russ treasured them above all the rest. They were of Ted Williams, Mickey Mantle, Leroy "Satchel" Paige, Lou Gehrig, Joe DiMaggio, and Jackie Robinson. Russell called them his "Special Six" and kept them wrapped in plastic in a wooden box. Everyone at Midbury Elementary knew about the Six, and many had gone over to Russell's house just to see them. The other boys had all given up trying to obtain the cards in trade, as Russ said he would rather part with his right arm (his pitching arm) than part with the Six. They were worth hundreds of dollars. If Russ were to sell his extensive baseball card collection, he would probably be the richest kid in school. Russ and his dad spent hours going over the collection together.

Marty wondered what it would be like to have a dad. He tried to remember his own

father, but couldn't. His parents had gotten a
divorce when he was just a year old, and his
father had moved away. Marty didn't even
know where he was living. "Somewhere
in the South," his mother had said. Marty
imagined that having a father would be like
having Gramps. But Gramps was probably
better than a father, he decided, because
Gramps was always doing special things
with him. Marty remembered the time they
made the bluebird house. Gramps said that
as soon as Mr. McGrath returned their ladder, he and Marty could hang the house outside Marty's bedroom window on the maple
tree.

"That way you'll wake up in the morning
watching bluebirds," Gramps said. "And the
first morning you'll see them, we'll celebrate,
because seeing a bluebird is an extraordinary
event and all extraordinary events must be cel-
ebrated."

"How will we celebrate?" Marty asked.

Gramps scratched his chin, and then his
eyes lit up. "By having breakfast in bed! That
is, if your bed will hold us both."

"It will, it will," Marty assured him. "But what will we have for breakfast?"

Gramps had to think for a minute. "How about blueberry pancakes?" He laughed. "Blue pancakes while we watch bluebirds." Marty had laughed too. Of course, Gramps had gotten sick before they had had a chance to hang the birdhouse and make the blue pancakes, but Marty could still remember what fun they had planning it all. Gramps knew how to make great plans. He knew more than most fathers, Marty supposed. Gramps knew all about Napoleon, and Vincent van Gogh, and all kinds of interesting people. And no one could tell a story like Gramps.

With a crampy feeling in his stomach, Marty remembered the day his mother told him that Gramps would be leaving.

"He needs to go to a hospital for an operation, and after that, he'll need to be in a nursing home," she had said. "I have to work all day, so there's no one to look after Gramps here. I found a good home. It's called Shady Maples, and they'll take good care of him there."

"But I can take care of him here," Marty had protested.

His mother smiled and shook her head. "You have to go to school all day," she reminded him.

"Why? Why do I have to go?" Marty had pleaded. "Why can't I stay home where Gramps can teach me? I already learn more from Gramps than I do in school."

But his mother had already called the nursing home, and after Gramps returned from the hospital, they had packed up his few belongings in three suitcases and a couple of boxes. Marty had helped put them in the car, but he didn't go with his mother and Gramps to the nursing home.

"You can come and visit once I'm settled in, Mars Bars," Gramps had said, trying to smile. But Marty knew that it wasn't a real smile. He tried to remember what Gramps's real smile looked like.

"I think my fingers are going to fall off." Russell's voice broke into Marty's thoughts. Marty looked at his friend and then down at his paper. He thought about Gramps and heard his gravelly voice saying, "All you have to do is concentrate, Mars Bars."

Marty put down his pencil and leaned over to untie his sneaker. He quickly slipped his foot out and pulled off his sock. Then he lifted his foot up to the desk, stuck his pencil between his toes, and used all his powers of concentration to write the letter *I*.

"Atta boy, Mars Bars." He imagined Gramps cheering him on as he slowly brought his toe down and up and then down and up again to form the letter *W*. It was twice as big as it should have been, but it was a *W* nonetheless.

"Marty," Russell whispered excitedly. "Hey, Marty!"

"Just a minute," Marty muttered, not looking up from his work. His powers of concentration were getting better all the time.

"But Marty . . . "

"Not now, Russ, I'm trying to concentrate," Marty whispered as he made a large, wavy *N*. He was concentrating so much that he hadn't even heard the door to the reading room open and close.

Suddenly a huge muscular arm swooped through the air and a few hairy fingers grabbed his ankle in an iron grip.

"Bellucci!" Mr. Bullner bellowed. "You're beginning to aggravate me, boy!"

Chapter 4

"I was . . . was . . . just . . . trying to . . ."
Marty stammered as Mr. Bullner unlocked his
grip.

"Never mind," Mr. Bullner snapped. "I
sent you two in here to write with your
hands, but since you're so preoccupied with
your *feet,* maybe you'd care to write about
them." A glint of pleasure shone in his nar-
row green eyes. His voice became smooth,
light, almost happy.

"After you finish the first sentence I gave
you, you can write this," Mr. Bullner continued. " 'I will keep my feet in my socks and
shoes where they belong.' Maybe you'll lose
interest in your feet after you write *that* one
hundred times."

Russell began to raise his hand, but put it down again when Mr. Bullner shot him a withering look.

"Yes, McGrath, that means you too," Mr. Bullner barked. "Perhaps you won't find Bellucci so entertaining after you've finished another writing assignment."

Marty looked over at his friend. He felt a pang of guilt. Then he looked at Mr. Bullner, who was nodding with satisfaction, his big hairy fingers caressing the whistle that hung from his neck. Marty cringed at the sight of the mean little grin on his red face. It was the kind of cold-hearted grin that comes when someone's glad that something bad is happening to someone else.

The moment the door to the reading room slammed shut, Marty whispered, "Another hundred sentences! If only I could have explained about the powers of concentration."

"If you keep coming up with these wacky ideas, we'll be stuck in here for a hundred years," Russell replied. "As it is, we'll probably miss recess all next week. Do you think he'd let us finish these at home, like home-work?"

"I don't know." Marty shrugged. "But I'm not going to ask him. Every time he looks at me, he thinks up a new sentence for me to write." Both boys decided it would be better to avoid Mr. Bullner as much as possible in the future.

"It's just our luck that the biggest, meanest teacher in the school hates us," said Marty.

"It's too bad we can't have plastic surgery on our faces," Russell mumbled as he started another sentence.

Mr. Bullner stopped in at the end of the period to collect the few sheets of paper that the boys had filled out. He stood shaking his head.

"I will see you two in this room the same time Monday and every day after that, until you've completed all two hundred sentences." He grinned just enough for the tips of his front teeth to show, and then he turned and walked toward the door.

Marty stared at the back of Mr. Bullner's bristly head. He squinted, trying to imagine what Mr. Bullner must have looked like as a ten-year-old. Try as he might, Marty couldn't. It was like trying to imagine how television works, or telephones. It seemed to be beyond his understanding. How could Mr. Bullner ever have been young?

Chapter 5

The gloom of the two hundred sentences hung over the two friends for the remainder of the day. Russell was still groaning about it as they stepped off the school bus. He and Marty lived next door to each other. Their houses were so close that the boys could wave to each other from their bedrooms.

Marty often went over to the McGrath house after school. With Gramps gone and Mrs. Bellucci away at work in the afternoons, the house felt as still and quiet as a tomb. The McGrath house, on the other hand, hummed with activity.

From the sidewalk, Marty could hear a blast of music coming from the McGraths' second floor. Russell's older sisters, Deena and

Megan, were waving at a high school boy from their bedroom windows. He was riding his bike down the street. Devin, Russell's little brother, was playing on the porch with his new kittens, Betty and Betina, while Harley, the McGraths' husky, barked from the kitchen. Mrs. McGrath was painting lawn furniture out on the grass in the side yard. She was talking to Mrs. Stapleford, a neighbor, who had stopped by to borrow some baking soda.

"Do you want to play Creeps in the Castle?" Marty asked. Creeps in the Castle was their favorite video game. Just then, Mrs. McGrath called, "Russell, hurry in and brush your teeth. You have a dentist appointment in fifteen minutes. And I want to take you shopping after that for some new shoes." Russell rolled his eyes and muttered, "I think I'd rather write another hundred sentences."

Marty headed for his empty house. He searched for the key his mother had left under the flowerpot on the porch. Since Gramps was no longer home to greet him, Marty had to let himself in. He pushed open the front door and stepped into the hall. The silence in the house still surprised him. Gramps had been away only two weeks. It seemed strange not to hear him shuffling about in his slippers, humming, or talking to Blubber, the goldfish in the bowl on the kitchen counter.

Marty went into the living room and threw himself down on the couch. He picked up the remote control and turned on the TV. Marty looked at the clock on the VCR. It would be two hours before his mother got home. He stared blankly at the cartoon figures that ran across the television screen. A big chicken was chasing a dog who was wearing a cowboy hat. Marty yawned. He had seen this cartoon a dozen times.

As he lay on the couch, he gazed around the room until he saw "the beast," which stood by the window. The beast was a big, shabby-looking chair, covered in worn velveteen material with green-and-gold flowers the size of dinner plates printed on it. The arms had become smooth with wear, and the footrest had a large rip that someone had tried to repair with coarse black thread. Bits of gray stuffing bubbled out between the long, irregular stitches. The beast was Gramps's chair. He had bought it several years ago at a garage sale for five dollars.

Marty smiled as he remembered the day Gramps had come home with it. Mrs. Bellucci was horrified as two high school boys carried the hulking piece of furniture to the window in the living room. The chair was so big that the boys had to move two end tables to make room for it.

"I have just purchased the chair of my dreams," Gramps announced dramatically, sitting down. As he stretched back, the footrest swung up with a loud creak. "Sitting in this chair will be the perfect way to end the day."

"But Pop, it's horrible!" Marty's mother gasped, coming into the room.

"No, Ann, it's a recliner," Gramps corrected her, winking at Marty.

"Pop, can't you see that it doesn't go with our other furniture? It's so big and so—so—awful!" she protested.

"But honey, you haven't heard the best part," Gramps said. He turned to Marty and pointed to the arm of the chair. "Mars Bars, come here and press this button," he commanded.

Marty walked to the chair and eagerly pressed a black button that was in a switch plate on the chair's left arm. Suddenly a man's voice sang out, "Ever since you left, I know that loving you too little is why you up and went. If only I had given . . ." The voice was coming from a speaker in the chair's headrest.

"Hey, that's neat," Marty said. "I never heard a chair sing before."

"Oh, that's so tacky," Marty's mother groaned.

Gramps was singing along with the refrain. "A hundred percent," he crooned, his eyes misting over. "Ah, the golden voice. Winston Tweedy. There was nobody like him. The fella that I bought the chair from was a big Tweedy fan too, and he rigged up this speaker with his favorite song."

"So why didn't he keep the chair himself?" Marty's mother asked.

"Oh, his wife got a new living room set, and he had to let it go. The poor guy. Can you believe my luck?" He turned to Marty and smiled. It was the smile of someone who had just opened the best Christmas present ever. "How often do you come across a musical chair in your life, hey, Mars Bars?" he asked, his eyes twinkling. "Once, maybe twice. And how often do you find a musical chair that actually plays one of your all-time favorite songs? Isn't it incredible?"

"Yeah, Gramps, it's incredible," Marty agreed, leaning on the chair's arm. He was waiting for the song to be over so he could push the button again.

"Pop, maybe you haven't noticed," Marty's mother called over the voice coming from the chair, "but *we* have new living room furniture too. And that thing is a monstrosity!"

"What's a monstrosity?" Marty wanted to know.

"It's a beast!" his mother exclaimed.

"It may be a beast," Gramps sighed dreamily. "But what a wonderful beast it is." He gave Marty a nod, and Marty climbed onto his lap. With big, sunny smiles, the two leaned back in the plush cushioned seat. Mrs. Bellucci huffed out of the room, Marty giggled, and Winston Tweedy continued to sing from deep within the chair.

From that day on, sitting in the beast became a standard bedtime ritual. Marty had to be in his pajamas with his teeth brushed before he was allowed on the chair. He would grab hold of the worn velvety arms and climb up into his grandfather's lap. Then with a great deal of ceremony Gramps would order him to push the "sacred button." Marty would giggle and press it, then he and Gramps would lean back and begin to sing along with the golden voice.

Gramps had explained to Marty that "One Hundred Percent" was a song "about doing your best, and giving all you have. It's the way I love you," Gramps said. "One hundred percent." After the song was over, Gramps told one of his stories about someone who had given his best and worked to see his dreams come true. Gramps told Marty that history was filled with such people, and he had an endless supply of stories about them. Gramps told wonderful stories about Ben Franklin, Napoleon, Frederick Douglass, Amelia Earhart, and more. Gramps and Marty both agreed that listening to the beast before bedtime was the perfect way to end the day.

After Gramps got sick, however, he spent most of his time in bed. He was too ill to sing or tell stories, and the chair had sat empty for a long while. Marty lay on the couch, staring into space. He got up and slowly walked across the room.

"Hello, Beast," he whispered, sinking into its soft cushioned seat. He sniffed the smoky gold-and-green flowers and closed his eyes. He could see Gramps sitting with his cigarette, a ring of smoke circling his bald head. For a moment, he could hear his grandfather's low, gravelly voice singing along with Winston Tweedy. Marty snuggled down into the soft velveteen.

He missed his grandfather's singing and the stories, so many stories. It was here in the chair that Marty had first heard about Napoleon. Suddenly Marty remembered his letter. He had left the one to Vincent van Gogh in his desk, but the letter to Napoleon was still in his back pocket. He pulled it out and read it over.

Miss Gerbino had looked confused when he'd explained why he wanted to write to Napoleon. Even his best friend, Russell, didn't understand why he would want to write to a dead person.

"You would understand, though, wouldn't you, Gramps?" Marty whispered out loud, letting the letter fall to his lap. But the only reply was the screeching of the chicken and the barking of the dog coming from the television set. Marty suddenly hated that cartoon, hated the fake voices, the fake barking, the empty house, the emptiness of the chair. How did this happen? How would his life ever seem right without Gramps?

Marty gently pushed the black button on the chair's arm. A tear rolled down his cheek and onto Napoleon's letter. He closed his eyes, burying his face in the velvety flowers as the golden voice began to sing, "Ever since you left . . ."

Chapter 6

"We're going to Shady Maples to visit Gramps tomorrow," Marty's mother told him that night. They were sitting at the kitchen table eating ice cream. Marty had spooned his chocolate chips onto his napkin, forming a little chocolate mountain. He always separated his food, preferring to eat one thing at a time. At supper he would separate the cucumbers and olives from his salad, eating first the lettuce, then the cucumber pieces, and finally the olives sitting beside his bowl. He looked up from his little pile of chocolate chips.

"Maybe Gramps feels better, and he'll be able to come home with us," Marty suggested. But his mother's eyes filled with tears.

"No, hon, I'm afraid Gramps won't be coming home," Mrs. Bellucci said softly. "You see, he's still very sick."

Marty stared down at his chocolate chip pile. It frightened him to see his mother so sad. He hated the thought of Gramps never coming home. He quietly took his spoon and mashed the chocolate chip mountain into his napkin.

"I know what," said his mother, wiping her eyes with her fingers. "Why don't we call Gramps tonight and say hello?"

Marty nodded. He was relieved to see his mother smile. He had never noticed until now how much she looked like Gramps. Her hair was brown and curly, while Gramps was almost bald, but they had the same soft brown eyes and their faces were the same round shape, though Gramps usually had a chinful of whiskers. His mother was wearing the crooked smile Marty had missed seeing during the past two weeks. It was Gramps's smile.

Marty watched as his mother dialed. After she talked to Gramps for several minutes, she handed Marty the receiver. His grandfather's gravelly voice seemed lower and weaker.

"So what have you been up to, Mars Bars?" Gramps asked.

"Not much," Marty answered.

"What are you doing in school?"

Marty thought for a minute. "We have to write a letter to a famous person," he said. He watched his mother walk to the refrigerator. "I wrote a letter to Napoleon," Marty whispered into the phone.

"A letter to Napoleon—now that's a great idea, Mars Bars!" Gramps said.

"It is?" Marty replied.

"Certainly it is," Gramps told him. "Napoleon was an amazing warrior."

"But the problem is, he's dead," Marty pointed out. "And Miss Gerbino said that I should write to someone who could answer my letter."

"But Napoleon *can* answer your letter," Gramps said.

"He can?"

"Yes." Gramps's voice had become a husky whisper. "Your mother tells me that the two of

you are coming tomorrow for a visit. Bring
your letter with you, and I'll see that it's
mailed."

"Mailed?" Marty repeated. "But to who,
Gramps? Who would you mail the letter to?"

"To Napoleon, of course," Gramps whispered. "Listen, Mars Bars, this is top secret. I
don't even want your mother to know, but
something strange and wonderful is going on
at Shady Maples. I can't tell you any more
now. Just bring the letter. Believe me, it will
get to Napoleon. I promise."

After saying good-bye, Marty handed the
phone to his mother and ran upstairs to his
bedroom. He flopped down on his bed and
pulled out the crumpled letter from his back
pocket.

"Something strange and wonderful is going
on at Shady Maples," he whispered his grandfather's words aloud. What? What did Gramps
mean? And what did the strange and wonderful thing have to do with his letter to Napoleon?

Marty's thoughts were interrupted by the
sudden rap of metal on glass and the tinkle of

a little bell. He ran to the window. He could see Russell standing in his bedroom. The clothesline that stretched from Marty's window to Russell's was barely visible in the darkness. Marty looked down and saw a small metal box fastened to the line with a metal clip. It was the box that carried their secret messages back and forth. Gramps had rigged up the message relay two summers ago, on Marty's birthday. It was the best present that Marty ever got. He and Russell rarely talked on the telephone or yelled across their yards to each other. Instead, they used their secret message system.

Marty opened the window and reached for the little box, unclipping the metal clasp. He opened the box, pulled out the note, and read the message:

Dear Avenger,

*Did you tell your mother about the two hun-
dred sentences? Don't! If my parents find out
about it, they will look like this:*

and then like this:

and I will look like this:

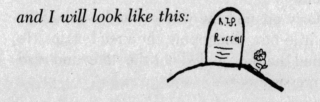

*What's new? How is special agent Measle? Is
he up to a night mission? Charlie is lonely and
could use some company.*

*Your friend,
The Flame*

The two friends used code names to sign their messages: Russell was the Flame and Marty was the Avenger. Marty went over to the cage on his dresser and took out his pet mouse, Measle. Last fall, when Marty had come down with the measles and had been cooped up in the house for days, Gramps had gone to the pet store and bought him a pet mouse.

"I can't believe you're bringing a rodent into our house," Marty's mother had said. (She didn't like mice, even cute little white ones.) "Wouldn't you rather have a new fish, Marty?" she suggested. "Maybe we could bring him back to the pet store and trade him for another goldfish."

But after taking one look at the soft white fur, the pink wrinkled nose, and the big, dark, pleading eyes, Marty knew that no fish could ever be as wonderful as Measle. (He had decided to call him Measle in honor of the disease.) Russell had talked his parents into getting him his own pet mouse after he had come down with the measles a week later. Russell had named his mouse Charlie.

The two mice, like their owners, had become great friends, visiting each other often via the clothesline. Marty and Russell referred to them as special agents, since they often traveled back and forth in the message box. If they were part of a night mission, they were allowed to sleep over in the other one's cage. It didn't seem to matter which cage they slept in, just as long as they were together. They would curl up cozily, wrapping their tails around each other before falling asleep.

Now Marty carefully opened the cage. The latch had broken several days ago. If Gramps had been home, he would have fixed it. Marty knew how Gramps loved to fix things. But Gramps was gone, so Marty used a piece of string to hold the door shut. Marty reached into the cage and gently picked up Measle.

"I'm sending you on another mission," he whispered, placing Measle in the metal box. The tiny white mouse sniffed all four corners before finally curling up into a little white ball. Marty put the lid on the box. (He and Gramps had drilled some air holes in the lid so the special agents could breathe.) Picking up his notebook from his desk, Marty ripped out a piece of paper. He pulled a pencil from his back pocket and sat down on his bed to write:

Dear Flame,
The two hundred sentences have been coded as strictly confidential info. Don't worry. New news also confidential. Something weird going on at Shady Maples (my gramps's nursing home.) Will check it out tomorrow and report any findings. Sending along special agent to spend the night.

Give him some water before he goes to sleep.

> *Your friend,*
> *The Avenger*

Later that night as Marty lay in bed, he couldn't stop thinking about Gramps and his letter to Napoleon.

If someone were dead, how was it possible

to send him a letter? Could he really write back? Marty snuggled into his pillow, listening to the pulley as the night wind whipped the clothesline back and forth outside his window. Over his bed, in a little wooden frame, his *Starry Night* picture twinkled in the moonlight. Marty closed his eyes and began to drift off to sleep, with the whisper of his grandfather's words still in his ear—*something strange and wonderful is going on at Shady Maples.*

Chapter 7

On Saturday morning, Marty and his mother made the two-hour drive to Shady Maples. As they walked up to the front doors, they passed a number of patients sitting in wheelchairs on the big white porch. It frightened Marty to see so many old and wrinkled people. He followed his mother into the lobby, and then on down the hall. A rancid odor like ammonia stung his nose. Marty tried not to gag. He could hear people moaning, and someone was crying.

"Martha? Where in the world has Martha gone?" a wavery voice called from one of the rooms. Marty quickened his step.

As they continued down the hall, they came upon a withered-looking woman, strapped into a wheelchair. She was the oldest person Marty had ever seen. She must be hundreds of years old, he thought. Her skin hung in papery ashen folds. A bright pink earring dangled from one drooping earlobe, while her silver wig hung, lopsided, over her other ear. Marty cringed when his mother stopped to say hello.

"How are you today?" Mrs. Bellucci asked cheerfully.

"I'm fine, thank you," answered the old woman creakily, nodding. "I saw a robin from my window this morning."

"Now that's a sure sign of spring," Marty's mother smiled.

"I know. And I have so much spring cleaning to do. But with the new baby here, it's hard to get everything done. Just keeping up with washing all the diapers is a chore."

Marty's mother shook her head as if she understood.

A tall, dark-haired nurse walked up to them. "Having a good morning, Lucy?" she asked, adjusting the old woman's wig.

"Yes, but there's so much to do now that the new baby is here," the old woman told her.

"Don't worry, everything will get done," the nurse said, smiling at Marty and his mother.

"Let's see about taking your medication now."
She grabbed hold of the chair and slowly
wheeled the old woman into her room.

"They don't have babies in this place, do
they?" Marty whispered as he and his mother
continued walking down the hall.

"No, she's just confused," his mother explained. "That happens sometimes when people get old. They start to relive their lives."

"Is that what's going to happen to Gramps?"
Marty asked, his eyes full of worry.

"I don't know, honey, but it doesn't happen
to everyone," his mother said. "If an old person becomes confused, this is a good place for
him or her to come. They can be taken care of
here." Marty looked away, the corners of his
mouth turning down.

Good? What was good about this place? Everyone was old and wrinkled, some of the people were crazy, and it smelled bad.

Marty stopped and looked behind him.
"Can I go wait in the car?" he asked.

"Oh, Marty, Gramps will be so disappointed
if you do that," his mother said. She took his
hand and led him into a large room.

There was a television set in one corner,

with couches and chairs around it. Walking past a bulletin board, Marty looked up to see the word BIRTHDAYS spelled out in big orange letters. Snapshots of old people in little party hats blowing out birthday candles were beneath the letters. Marty thought it looked strange to see such old faces beneath the brightly colored hats. He was relieved that none of the old people were in the room. He followed his mother to a couch and sat down.

"Marty, this is where Gramps lives now," his mother began. "I know it seems strange to see so many old people all together. I felt the same way when I first came here. But right now it's the best place for Gramps, because there are nurses to take care of him. He's going to be here for a long time, Marty, and if you don't visit him, he'll feel very sad. I know it's hard for you, but for Gramps's sake, do you think you can do it?"

Marty bit down on his lip. For Gramps he thought he could do just about anything. "Okay," he whispered.

Marty's mother smiled. "That's my boy," she said, taking hold of his hand. "You know that your grandfather is a special kind of person. He sees good in so many things, Marty, even when things look bad to us. He needs to see the good in things here. We mustn't remind him of what's wrong with this place."

"But what if he misses us? What if he's lonely here?" Marty asked, fighting back tears.

His mother squeezed his hand. "Your gramps makes friends wherever he goes. He needs an audience for all his stories. I'm sure he's made quite a few friends already. And besides, we're here today to visit him, and we'll come back as often as we can, okay?"

"Okay," Marty mumbled. Together they walked back out to the hall. "There's 227," said Mom, pointing to the left. "That's Gramps's room."

Marty followed his mother into the room and saw Gramps asleep in a bed by the window. He was wearing the blue-and-yellow pajamas Marty and his mother had bought him for Christmas last year. Marty stared at his grandfather from the end of the bed. Gramps didn't look the same. He looked smaller, thinner, shrunken. The skin on his freckled hands looked transparent. Marty wished he could go back to the car before his grandfather woke up. Mom leaned over and gave Gramps a kiss.

Marty stopped breathing as Gramps opened his eyes and blinked several times. Then the old man turned his head and began to smile. It was the same crooked smile that Marty remembered so well. "So you made it, Mars Bars," Gramps said in his own wonderful gravelly voice. "It's good to see you both."

"Oh, Pop, it's so good to see you," Marty's mother said, bursting into tears. She reached over and hugged her father. Marty took a step backward, not knowing what to do.

"It's okay, hon," Gramps whispered, stroking his daughter's hair as she continued to cry. "It's going to be okay."

"Are they treating you all right? Is it comfortable enough?" asked Mom as she tried to regain her composure.

"They're treating me fine," Gramps assured her.

Marty's mother went on to ask him dozens of questions concerning his diet, medication, and vitamins. "And mail. Are you getting your mail? Did you get the care package I sent you last Tuesday?" she asked.

Gramps nodded. "There's an amazing mail-room here," he said, winking at Marty. Marty suddenly remembered his letter to Napoleon. He reached into his back pocket and pulled out the crumpled piece of paper. His grandfather's reddened eyes seemed to light up at the sight of it. He smiled mischievously at Marty, then turned to Marty's mother, a worried look coming over his face.

"Those cookies you sent were delicious, Ann, but I'm wondering, what with this new medication I've been taking, if I should eat chocolate, you know, because of the caffeine. Do you think you could go speak to one of the nurses about it?"

"Of course, Pop." Marty's mother sprang up from the bed. "Marty, you stay here and visit with Gramps while I go to the nurses' station. I won't be long."

Gramps tapped the blanket beside him, and Marty sat down on the bed.

"Hugs first," Gramps whispered. They hugged for a long time. Marty noticed right

away how different Gramps was. He was skin-
nier, his neck smelled funny, and his hands
were trembling more than ever. Still, Marty
felt a wave of relief as he hugged him once
more.

"I brought the letter, just like you told me
to," Marty said, handing him the crumpled
piece of paper.

"So you have," Gramps mumbled, reaching
for the thick-lensed glasses that lay on a table
beside the bed. He slowly read the letter.
"Nice of you to mention your old gramps to
the great man." He chuckled. "And I like your
drawing. That's a fine palm tree. The emperor
will like it too, I'm sure."

"But Gramps, when you said that you could
mail the letter to Napoleon, you were just kidding, right?" Marty asked.

Gramps shook his head. "Meant every
word," he whispered.

Marty looked him in the eye. "It's not just a
story, like the time you told me the ocean was
drying up because all the fish were drinking
the water, is it, Gramps? Or the time you said
Santa Claus's sled had broken down, so he'd
be delivering presents in a pickup truck. For

weeks, I expected to see Santa Claus every time a red pickup truck went by. It's not like one of those stories, is it, Gramps?"

The old man frowned. "I admit I've told some whoppers in my day, but I promise, this isn't one of them." He looked around to be sure that no nurses were out in the hall within hearing distance. Then he turned back to Marty. "You can still keep a secret, can't you?"

Marty nodded. "Can I tell Russ, though?"

"Okay, but only Russell," Gramps answered. "Now listen. Shady Maples has two mailrooms. One is an ordinary kind of mailroom in which mail gets delivered to ordinary living people, and the other . . ." He paused.

"And the other?" Marty asked.

"The other," Gramps whispered, leaning closer, "the other is Henry Cooper's Secret Courier Service. From his mailroom you can send a letter anywhere in the world, anywhere in time. This letter," he said excitedly, waving Marty's letter in the air, "can and will be sent to Napoleon."

"But who is Henry Cooper, and how . . ." Marty sputtered.

"He's a resident here." Gramps was talking

faster, trying to say everything before Marty's mother returned. "Henry Cooper is an old fellow now, but he worked as a mailman for forty years and was always interested in travel. Since he worked for the post office, time has always been important to him. Time travel became a sort of hobby that he says he just fell into."

"But how does he do it? Travel in time, I mean?" Marty asked.

"I'm not really sure myself," Gramps said. "All I know is Henry Cooper has found a way to deliver the mail to anyone, anywhere in time." He winked at Marty. "Some mailman, hey, Mars Bars?"

Mrs. Bellucci came back, and the conversation abruptly returned to normal things, like medications, vitamins, and food. Marty and his mother stayed for most of the day, but when Gramps began to yawn, Mrs. Bellucci decided it was time to leave.

"How about a kiss good-bye for the old man?" Gramps asked. Marty leaned over and kissed his cheek. Gramps reached out and with trembling hands pulled him toward him in a hug.

Marty's eyes filled with tears. "I don't want you to have to stay here all alone, Gramps!" he cried. "I want you to come home with us!"

"You know I'd like nothing better than to do just that," Gramps said, holding him tight. "But there's a time for everything. And now is the time for me to be here."

"But why do you have to be so far away?" Marty asked, brushing the tears from his cheek.

"Far away? I'm not far away, Mars Bars, and you're not, either. Why, I've got you right here," Gramps said, pointing to his head. "And right here." He pointed to his heart. "This place may not be the Ritz, but it's not so bad, really. Besides," he whispered in Marty's ear, "I've got to stay here and see about a certain letter getting posted, now, don't I?"

Marty smiled through his tears. Good old Gramps, still telling his stories. He reached over and gave his grandfather one last hug good-bye. As sad as Marty felt at leaving Gramps behind, he couldn't stop thinking about Henry Cooper and his mysterious mailroom. It certainly sounded like Gramps was telling the truth. But he always sounded that way when he told one of his stories.

There's probably no such person as Henry Cooper living here, Marty told himself as he and his mother walked down the hall. Still, he peeked into every room they passed, hoping to see just such a person.

"Gramps looked so glad to see you," Marty's mother said after they got into their car and were driving out of the parking lot.

"Um," Marty mumbled, staring out the window.

"What were you two gabbing about when I came back from the nurses' station, anyway? It got awfully quiet when I walked into the room."

Marty turned to look at an old pickup truck that was parked on the side of the road. It was red. It was empty. Marty smiled. Santa must have run out of gas, he thought. Then he turned to his mother, who was waiting for an answer to her question.

"Oh, you know Gramps," Marty sighed. "He loves telling loony stories."

I just wish one of those loony stories would

come true, Marty thought, as they drove farther down the highway. Well, that's not going
to happen this time, he told himself, now that
I'm ten years old and not a little kid anymore.
Marty tried thinking of other things, of Russ,
and Measle and Charlie, but as he closed his
eyes and leaned back on the seat, he heard
Gramps's whisper.

"Some mailman, hey, Mars Bars?" Suddenly Marty Bellucci, the big ten-year-old,
found himself wishing and hoping with all his
heart that, hidden away at Shady Maples, an
old mailman by the name of Henry Cooper
was posting a letter to Napoleon.

Chapter 8

Two weeks later, a letter from Andrea Markoff to Jessica Hollander was delivered to Midbury Elementary School. Jessica grinned, Miss Gerbino grinned, and the secretary who delivered the letter from the office grinned. Everyone laughed and talked as Jessica opened the envelope. But there was no signed picture of Andrea Markoff. Marty could see that the ballet star's reply was a form letter. The only thing handwritten was Jessica's name after the *Dear.*

"She must send out the same letter to hundreds of fans," Marty whispered to Russell after inspecting the letter.

"At least Jessica got a letter back," Russell said. He was still waiting for a reply from Ken

Griffey, Jr. Russell looked at Marty's long face. "I told you to write to someone who was alive. Do you really believe some weird old mailman, traveling through time, is going to deliver your letter to Napoleon?"

Marty shrugged. He was feeling less and less hopeful. Actually, he was beginning to doubt more and more that a person named Henry Cooper even existed, much less traveled through time delivering mail. Marty looked around the room. There were twenty-one people still waiting for letters, not including himself. He slumped in his seat. He knew he would have to watch the same twenty-one people receive important letters, and then listen to the letters being read aloud in class.

Maybe Russ was right. Maybe I should have written to somebody who was alive, Marty thought as he watched Jessica dance up to the front of the room. She read her letter out loud, squealing every now and then.

On Tuesday, Tim Torrenti received a letter from the president of the United States. Tim grinned, Miss Gerbino grinned, and Miss Pessin, the principal, grinned. There was talk that Tim might be asked to read his letter aloud to the entire school over the intercom.

"It's just another form letter, probably run off on a computer," Marty whispered to Russell. "The White House must send out millions of them." Russ nodded in agreement, but couldn't resist touching the letter all the same.

"Way to go, Tim-o!" Patrick Huvey and Danny Reece cheered. Everyone seemed to be glad for Tim. Now everyone looked forward to the important letters that were arriving daily. There were letters from famous actors, writers, and athletes.

When Ken Griffey, Jr., sent Russell a letter along with a glossy black-and-white photograph, Russell was so excited, his hands shook as he read his letter aloud. There was a handwritten P.S. that said, "Your baseball card collection sounds great. Hang on to those Special Six."

Marty was glad for his friend, but he was beginning to feel stupid for having written to a dead person and for actually believing that Gramps's story was true.

On Monday the secretary from the office

stopped in the classroom with an envelope addressed to Melanie Minrow. The governor of New Hampshire's return address was printed in blue and gold on the envelope's top-left side. Miss Gerbino smiled, the secretary smiled, and Melanie smiled as she jumped out of her chair to collect her letter.

Each day that the secretary walked into their classroom with a big smile on her face and an important letter in her hand, Marty cringed. He was beginning to hate the sight of her because he knew that neither the smile nor the letter would be for him.

On Friday morning, everyone in class had his or her science book open. The class had just read the first chapter, on electricity.

"Who was the 'Wizard of Menlo Park' and what was he famous for?" Miss Gerbino asked the class. Danny Reece's hand shot up. Miss Gerbino nodded in his direction.

"The Wizard of Menlo Park was Thomas Alva Edison, and he had his laboratory in Menlo Park, New Jersey," Danny answered. "And he invented light." Everyone laughed at this answer.

"I mean the light bulb," Danny quickly added.

"That's right," Miss Gerbino said. "But was he a real wizard with potions and spells?"

Marty raised his hand. "No," he said. "He was just a person with good ideas." He looked over at Russell and winked.

"And good luck," Russell added, winking back.

"That's true," Miss Gerbino agreed. "And I just happen to have twenty-three light bulb stickers, which I will hand out in honor of the Wizard of Menlo Park after we finish with to-day's lesson." Everyone oohed and aahed. Marty smiled. He loved the way Miss Gerbino made schoolwork so much fun, talking about wizards and giving out stickers.

"All right, what else can you tell me about Thomas Edison?" Miss Gerbino asked, looking around the room.

"After he became famous, he moved his lab to West Orange, New Jersey," Tricia Horta said. "My grandmother lives in New Jersey," she added proudly.

"That's interesting, Tricia. And who can tell

me what else, besides the electric light, Mr.
Edison is credited with inventing?" Marty
raised his hand.

"The phonograph," he said.

"Yes, and what else?" Miss Gerbino asked.

"The electric chair!" Russell called out.
Some of the girls groaned at this, and some of
the boys laughed.

"What else?" Miss Gerbino wanted to know.

"The electric locomotive," Lindsey Walren
said. They went on and on, with everyone calling out Thomas Edison's inventions. It was
soon obvious why he was called the Wizard of
Menlo Park.

Then the secretary opened the door, and
the room suddenly grew quiet.

"Here we go again," Marty groaned under
his breath. He was about to look back at his
science book to see what else Thomas Edison
had invented, when he noticed something different. The secretary wasn't smiling. In fact,
she seemed to be frowning as she handed a
long gray envelope to Miss Gerbino. Miss
Gerbino looked curiously at the fancy black
printing on the envelope.

"To Martin Bellucci, Midbury Elementary School." She read the words aloud. Marty looked at Russell, whose mouth had dropped open. Miss Gerbino went on to read the return address. "From the Emperor Napoleon Bonaparte." Now Marty's mouth dropped open too as Miss Gerbino read the postmark: "Paris, France." A deeper hush fell over the classroom, followed by a wave of whispers.

"Isn't he dead?" the secretary asked. Miss Gerbino nodded and motioned for Marty to come up to the front of the room. She had a dazed expression on her face as she handed him the envelope. He looked down and ran his finger over the words that Napoleon Bonaparte had written in fancy script.

He turned the envelope over to find a stamped design in a burgundy-colored wax, with the letter N in the center of it. He looked up at Miss Gerbino, not knowing what to do.

"That's how letters were sealed long ago." Miss Gerbino's voice had become no more than a whisper. She looked as confused as the secretary, who stood beside her. "You have to break the seal to open it," she said. Marty quickly slipped his finger under the wax and pulled it off, then opened the envelope. No one spoke as he pulled out a crisp piece of yellowish parchment paper. This was no form letter that had been run off on a computer. The fine black script had been written in ink. There was another decorative seal with the emblem of an eagle at the bottom of the letter next to the signature. This one, however, seemed to be made of gold. With trembling fingers, Marty held up the letter and began to read aloud.

Monsieur Bellucci,

Thank you for your kind letter and concern. As you can see, each day brings fresh rumors of my death spread by my enemies. It is true that death's cold embrace waits for me at every turn. But as all the world is my witness, I will never bow to cowardice. No, Monsieur Bellucci, if you have followed my course, you will see that the armor I wear to fend off the arrows and slings of my enemies is of no ordinary meld. No, the armor that shields my chest is wrought of courage, de-

termination, loyalty. Under such a mantle my heart continues to beat strong, for it is the mantle of glory I wear so proudly, monsieur, the mantle of France!

By the way, I was most happy to hear that someone has thought to name a sweet after me. Can you tell me, does this confection have chocolate as one of its ingredients? After years of holding strong in battle and standing firm against the onslaught of my foes, I must confess that I have a pitiful weakness for such sweets. As for my stay on Elba, there is very little chocolate to be had here, and so you can well imagine my distress. And yes, I have sighted sharks, but truthfully, they disturb me less than the bloodthirsty creatures who plot to bring down my empire. I am sending this letter on to Paris, where my secretary has instructions to post it to you.

Veuillez agréer, Monsieur, l'expression de mes sentiments distingués,

Napoleon Bonaparte
l'Empereur de la France

(My family called me Rabulione when I was a boy, meaning the "one who never minds his own business"!)

Marty looked up from the letter to see Russ's startled face. The two friends stared at each other.

Oh my gosh! Marty was thinking. Henry Cooper must have delivered my letter. Gramps was telling the truth. He was really telling the truth!

Chapter 9

"I don't understand, Marty." Miss Gerbino shook her head. "Did your letter actually get mailed?"

Marty gulped. "Yes."

"But Marty, to whom? To whom was the letter mailed?" Miss Gerbino asked.

"To Napoleon," Marty said truthfully.

Miss Gerbino and the secretary exchanged astonished looks.

"Then who wrote back to you?" the secretary wondered aloud.

"Someone living in Paris, France, from the looks of the postmark," Miss Gerbino said, peering at the envelope in her hand. It took a long while for the class to settle down after the excitement of the letter. A few people, including Miss Gerbino, asked to reread the letter several times before the day's end.

On the school bus later that afternoon, everyone seemed to have an opinion about the incredible letter.

"The whole thing is a joke, if you ask me," Danny Reece said, leaning into the aisle from his seat. "I'd be embarrassed if I were you, Marty. Now the whole school knows that you were dumb enough to try and send a letter to a dead person. You probably got your mother or somebody to write the letter."

"If his mother wrote the letter, how do you explain the postmark from Paris, France?" Russell quickly came to his friend's defense.

"Maybe Bellucci is such a mama's boy that his mother didn't want to disappoint him, so she got on an airplane and went to France to mail the letter," snickered Kyle Henly, who was sitting next to Danny. Everyone except Marty and Russell laughed at this last remark.

"You're just jealous because you didn't get a letter from Napoleon!" Russell shouted.

"Hey, Mickey Mouse McGrath!" Kyle

shouted back. "Haven't you heard? Dead people don't write letters."

"Oh, no?" Russ asked, his face reddening to the color of his hair. "Well, you don't know everything. If Marty says the letter's from Napoleon, I believe it's from Napoleon. And I bet he can write to whoever he wants and get a letter back."

"Even if they're dead?" Robbie Weston yelled.

"Even if they're dead!" Russell yelled back. Marty was about to open his mouth when Danny Reece suddenly spoke up.

"Okay, Russ, let's make a bet. I'll bet you six of my best baseball cards, for your Special Six, that Marty can't write to a dead man and get a letter back."

"Now wait a minute," Marty protested, but he was shouted down by Russell, who was leaning over Marty's seat into the aisle.

"You're on, Danny!" Russell cried above the uproar as everyone started calling out the names of dead people that Marty could write to.

"George Washington! King Tut! Abraham Lincoln!" they shouted.

"Come on, Russ, this is our stop," Marty said, looking out the window. He picked up his book bag and lunchbox. Russell got to his feet and silently walked down the aisle.

"So long, Mickey Mouse McGrath," Danny called. "So long, Mama's Boy."

"Just ignore him. Just ignore him," Marty whispered as he followed Russ to the front of the bus. But he could see Russell's free hand tightening into a fist as Danny continued to taunt them.

"Mickey Mouse McGrath and Mama's Boy . . ." They were almost to the bus door when Russell turned and yelled at Danny Reece.

"Abraham Lincoln!"

"What about him?" Danny cried.

"I'll bet that Marty can get a letter from Abraham Lincoln." Everyone started jeering and hooting. Even Tony, the bus driver, laughed. Marty groaned and shoved his friend forward until they had finally made it down the bus steps to the sidewalk.

"The bet is on, and you can kiss the Special Six good-bye!" Danny called from a window as the bus pulled away.

"Why did you have to go and bet on the Six?" Marty grumbled.

"I don't know," said Russell, with a dazed look on his face. "It just happened so fast. I never meant that I would really . . . Oh no, what if I lose? Marty, I can't lose, can I?" he cried.

Marty made a face and kicked a stone as they began to walk down the sidewalk. "I don't know. I guess not."

"You guess not!" Russell exclaimed. "Marty, I can't lose the Special Six. They're the best thing I'll ever own in my whole entire life. I'll die if I lose the Special Six!"

"Calm down, calm down," Marty said.

As they neared the McGraths' house, they saw Russ's older sister Deena standing on their front porch.

"Russ, Mom wants you to hurry up," she called. "Grandma is here, and we're taking pictures of everyone. Hurry up and get in here."

"Don't worry, I'll send you a message later tonight," Marty told Russ. He walked next door to his house and unlocked the front door.

He headed straight for the living room, where he flung himself down on the beast. Instead of turning on the television, Marty pressed the little black button. The golden voice poured out from the headrest. "When somebody loves you . . ."

Marty smiled and reached into his book bag, pulling out the crisp parchment paper from the long gray envelope.

"'Monsieur Bellucci.'" He read his name at the beginning of the letter and grinned. "Henry Cooper is for real, and he can really deliver mail anywhere and to anyone in time! Wow!" he whispered aloud.

Napoleon could have been on the island of Elba when he got my letter, Marty decided. Gramps had told him that Napoleon had been exiled on Elba but had escaped and returned to France in triumph. He went to war again and died a prisoner on the island of St. Helena.

Marty closed his eyes and fell asleep with his head resting against the soft velveteen headrest. After a while, he began to dream. He heard the rustling of palm trees in the wind. He could see the waves of a white-capped ocean breaking under a brilliant blue sky. He knew it was the sky of Elba. Along the shore, he could see a little white cottage nestled among the glowing green palms.

Marty walked into the cottage and saw Napoleon, in full military dress, sitting at a little wooden table. The tabletop was strewn with maps. Napoleon was busy poring over the maps, plotting his army's next battle.

Suddenly there was a knock at the cottage door, and Napoleon got up to answer it. A little withered old woman floated over the doorway, dangling from a huge green silk balloon that was attached to her shoulders. It was Lucy, the old woman from the nursing home.

A strange flying contraption was strapped to the old woman's back. Two huge papery blue wings fanned out from a network of brass gears and pulleys. One pink earring dangled from her left ear, while her other was partly covered by her curly gray wig. She was covered from head to toe with fine silver dust. With twinkling eyes and a shy smile, she brushed the silvery filaments from her arms.

"Delivery for His Majesty, Napoleon Bonaparte," Lucy announced in a creaky voice. "Care of Henry Cooper's Secret Courier Service." She reached into a big leather mailbag that hung from her shoulder and pulled out a letter. Napoleon turned to Marty and nodded.

"I'm so glad that you wrote back," Napoleon said. "It has been lonely, and I do enjoy a good letter. But since you've also decided to visit, why not come and help me plan my next battle?" He stood waiting, his finger pointing to the table strewn with maps. Marty could hardly believe his ears.

"Help me plan my next battle . . . help me plan my next battle . . ."

"Wake up, Marty. Wake up, come on, you can help me set the table." Marty opened his eyes and to his great disappointment Napoleon was no longer standing before him. Instead, Mrs. Bellucci, dressed in the frumpy blue bathrobe she always put on when she came home from work, was pointing to the table in the kitchen.

"Mom, when did you get home?" Marty asked.

"I've been home for twenty minutes, sleepy-head. I've already taken my shower, and I could use some help setting the table for supper." She turned and walked into the kitchen.

Marty rubbed his eyes and yawned. Then he stood up, stuffing Napoleon's letter into his book bag. Marty wondered if he should tell his mother about the letter. He wished he could, but he didn't want to have to tell her about Gramps and Henry Cooper. He decided not to mention it for now.

That night, secret messages flew fast and furiously across the line from the Flame to the Avenger and from the Avenger back to the Flame.

Dear Avenger,

Have you written the letter to A. Lincoln yet? You know I can't lose that bet. Send me Napoleon's letter so I can read it again. How do you think Henry Cooper goes back in time? Does he have some kind of time machine–mail truck? Why don't you write to The Guinness Book of World Records? You could be the first kid to ever get a letter from a dead person.

I'm sending along Charlie, but don't let him loose in your room. He's been bad, eating pillow stuffing again and nibbling on the end of my new blanket.

Your friend,
The Flame

Dear Flame,

I don't know how Henry Cooper travels through time. I've been thinking a lot about it. Maybe he invented some kind of special stamp that gives off a light, and once the light shines on him, it transports him back in time. Or maybe he's got some kind of beam machine like on Star Trek.

I can't write to The Guinness Book of World Records *because I promised my gramps that I would keep Henry Cooper a secret. I'm not supposed to tell anyone except you. So remember, we can't tell anyone else, not even Miss Gerbino. Tomorrow, my mom and I are going back to visit Gramps. I hate having to go back to Shady Maples, because it smells bad and everyone is so old there, but I have to visit my gramps. Maybe he will show me Henry Cooper's mailroom! Measle has been squeaking for an hour. I think he knew that Charlie was coming over to spend the night.*

Your friend,
The Avenger

P.S. *I still don't know if it's a good idea to write to Abraham Lincoln. What if Miss Gerbino starts asking more questions? I promised Gramps I'd keep his secret.*

Dear Avenger,
   If I lost my dad's six best baseball cards, I'd look like this:

And I'd have to do this:

It was because of you that I made that stupid bet anyway. All you have to do is write one more letter. Don't worry about Miss Gerbino. Have A. Lincoln send the letter to your house instead of the school. You're always home before your mom, so you can get the letter and bring it to school.

Here is your Napoleon letter back. It is probably the best letter a kid ever got in the whole world.

The Flame

P.S. But not as good as a letter from Abraham Lincoln!

Marty dropped the Flame's last note onto his desk and checked on Measle and Charlie. They were snuggling up to each other in Measle's cage and softly squeaking.

"What are you two gabbing about?" Marty wondered aloud as he gently tapped on the cage with his fingers. "I bet I know. Charlie, you're probably telling Measle all about your blanket nibbling, and Measle, you're telling Charlie all about the adventure you had under my bed last night, and how you ate almost a whole bag of Gummy Worms. Well, as far as mouse news goes, that's okay, but now I'll give you a little people news. Did you know that I got a letter from the emperor Napoleon today?" Charlie blinked and Measle hiccuped on hearing the news.

"I knew you'd be excited," Marty said as he turned off his light and flopped down on his bed with a yawn. "Now, what do you think I should write to Abraham Lincoln?" he whispered, snuggling under his blankets.

Chapter 10

Martin Bellucci
140 Elmstead Street
Midbury, New Hampshire 03301

Dear President Lincoln,

I hope you don't mind my writing to you, but it's important. My friend Russell made a bet with Danny Reece that if I wrote to you, you would write back. Russell is my best friend, and I would feel bad if he lost the bet on account of me. It's a long story, but I really do need you to write me a letter. It doesn't have to be a long one.

My gramps told me a little bit about you. He said that you were a fair and honest president. He also said that when you were a boy, you walked twenty miles to get to school each day.

My mom runs every day so that she can lose weight. My friend Russ and I don't walk to school. We ride. Russ is the skinniest person I know. If he had to walk twenty miles to school, he would probably get so skinny, he would disappear!

If my gramps were living twenty miles away, I would try and walk to see him. But he's one hundred and ten miles away, so I can't. I'd be really glad if you could write back to me, because a lot of the kids at school are making fun *of me now and calling me names. If Gramps were here, I could ask him what to do about it. It's hard to feel good when kids are calling you names.*

> *Your friend,*
> *Martin "Mars Bars" Bellucci*

"Mom, do you have an envelope?" Marty called into the bathroom on Saturday morning. His mother was standing at the sink, blow-drying her hair.

"Look in the desk drawer!" she yelled over the noise of the dryer. "There should be some stamps in there, too."

What kind of a stamp would it take to send a letter a hundred years back in time? Marty wondered as he ran down the stairs. He skipped the last two steps and opened the desk drawer. After finding the envelope and sealing his letter to Abraham Lincoln, Marty stuck it in his backpack along with Napoleon's letter and walked into the kitchen.

"Hurry up and fix yourself a bowl of cereal. We'll be leaving for Shady Maples soon," Mrs.

Bellucci called from upstairs. As Marty poured some cereal into a bowl, he couldn't help thinking about the nursing home and how much he hated it. If only Gramps didn't have to stay there. Marty frowned as he started picking the raisins out of his cereal.

"So, who are you writing to?" his mother asked, coming into the room. Marty looked up, not knowing what to say. The phone rang, and Mrs. Bellucci picked it up.

"Hello," she said, still looking at Marty.

"Abraham Lincoln," Marty said as softly as he could.

"Um, that's nice," she mouthed the words as she nodded in his direction. Marty could see that his mother was busy listening to the person on the phone. He hoped that it would be such an interesting call, his mother would forget about his letter. It was, and she did.

Marty became absorbed in playing with the raisins. At first he pretended that each raisin was a brick. He lined them up, making a long sidewalk. Then he decided that the raisins were alive and had personalities. There was a little fat one that Marty named Bubba, and a skinny, twisted one that he called Skeeter. Bubba and Skeeter were brothers, and they had a big family of aunts and uncles and cousins. Marty carefully picked them all out of his bowl. They were a family of acrobatic raisins, he decided, and he began to stack them up, one on top of another, for their famous family pyramid trick.

"Hey, Bubba, give me a hand," Marty whispered, lifting Skeeter over the pile.

"Very funny, Skeeter." Marty lowered his voice. "You know raisins don't have hands."

"That was Shady Maples," said his mother, hanging up the phone. "Mrs. Furness, the social director, just wanted to ask about Gramps's birthday next month. They certainly seem to care about the residents."

Marty shrugged. He was beginning to feel queasy about having to go back to the nursing home. "It still smells," he said, placing Skeeter's little sister, DeeDee, on top of the heap. It looked more like a heap now than a pyramid.

"It wasn't that bad." Mrs. Bellucci sighed as she stood in front of the refrigerator. "And you

know how much Gramps is looking forward to
seeing you. Oh, and Mrs. Furness mentioned
that today is Pet Day. Visitors bring in all kinds
of pets for the residents to look at and hold. It's
a nice way for the old people to get in touch
with animals again. You know how Gramps
loves animals." Her voice suddenly turned
naggy. "Marty, please stop playing with your
food and finish your breakfast. I'd like to leave
for the home before ten."

Mrs. Bellucci's back was to him as she stood
at the counter, counting out vitamins. Marty
quickly placed the last raisin relative on the
heap. It was Bubba's grandmother. The mountain of raisins wobbled. Bubba's grandmother
was not a skinny raisin. Bubba's grandmother
was downright plump. The pyramid came
crashing down, with several raisins silently
rolling off the table and onto Mrs. Bellucci's
chair.

"Will you hurry up and finish eating that
cereal?" Mrs. Bellucci said, pulling out the
chair and sitting down. "Why do you have to
make such a big production out of every
meal?"

"Why did you have to sit on Bubba's grand-mother?" Marty replied, shoving a spoonful of cereal into his mouth.

"What? What did you say about a grand-mother?"

"Lots of grandmothers." Marty nodded his head up and down. "I bet there are lots of grandmothers in that place—you know, Shady Maples." Before his mother could question him further, he slurped down the rest of his cereal and bounded from the table, running into the hall.

"Remember to brush your teeth!" his mother called as he climbed the stairs. "And make your bed, and put away those toys on your rug, and . . ."

Marty closed his bedroom door, hoping to shut out the commands that had followed him up the stairs. He knew that once his mother got going, she could think of hundreds of pic-ayune things for him to do. She had rattled off a list of commands for him and Gramps so often, Gramps had come to the conclusion that her lists were written by some voodoo priest who sent them to her via brain waves.

"When a woman can think of that many jobs for a man to do, there's got to be black magic involved," Gramps had often said. "She starts and she can't stop. It's a black magic thing, and the only way we can protect ourselves is to hide." So he and Marty would sneak into the garage, with Marty giggling as Gramps turned on the radio to drown out the voodoo commands.

"I wish you were here to help me ward off the voodoo now, Gramps," Marty whispered aloud.

Standing at his open window, he suddenly heard Russell and his little brother, Devin, shouting. He looked over at Russell's bedroom and saw the two having a pillow fight. As usual, Devin was getting clobbered.

Often Marty wished that he could have a little brother to clobber. He wouldn't clobber him hard or anything, just enough to make him laugh. Devin always laughed at first but usually ended up in tears. Marty could hear him beginning to whimper now as Russ's pillow came down on his head.

Marty walked over to his dresser and tapped on Measle's cage. He was glad he had Measle to talk to. Whenever he felt lonely, Measle could always cheer him up. As he stood watching Measle and Charlie nibbling on one of their toys, Marty thought of Gramps again. He wondered what he did when he got lonely at Shady Maples. Suddenly Marty remembered his mother telling him about Pet Day, and he got a great idea.

"Of course!" Marty cried out loud. "I'll bring Measle and Charlie to visit Gramps for Pet Day." Then he raced down the stairs to ask his mother. She was standing at the kitchen sink, washing dishes.

"Oh, I don't know if that's such a good idea." Mrs. Bellucci made a face.

"Why not?" Marty demanded. "They're trained and they would stay in their cage and Gramps would love to see them. I know he would."

"Well, all right. If you promise to be responsible and keep an eye on them every minute. But you'll have to ask Russell's permission to take Charlie."

Marty's eyes opened wide as another great idea came to him.

"Russ can come with us!" he exclaimed.

"Russ can come too!" Suddenly the dreaded visit to Shady Maples was becoming a wonderful adventure. As Marty thought about how he and Russell could go off in search of the secret mailroom together, he whooped with glee.

An hour later, the Bellucci house stood empty and silent, and Bubba's grandmother lay flattened on a kitchen chair. Meanwhile the Bellucci car was heading down the highway to Shady Maples. In the front seat, Mrs. Bellucci hummed along to the radio, while in the backseat, the Avenger and the Flame kept their voices low as they whispered about letters and bets and secret mailrooms. And on the floor in his cage, Special Agent Measle kept watch as his fellow agent, Charlie, silently nibbled away at the string latch on the cage door.

Chapter 11

When they first arrived at the nursing home, Mrs. Bellucci went directly to the nurses' desk and sent Marty and Russell ahead to visit with Gramps.

"Tell Gramps I want to speak with the nurses about his test results. I'll be there in a minute," she told them. Marty led Russell down the long hallway.

"You were right about the smell," Russell whispered.

"Yeah, but you get used to it after a while," Marty said, shifting Measle's cage from his left hand to his right. When they reached room 227, Marty was surprised to see Gramps sitting in a wheelchair by the side of his bed. Marty had never seen his grandfather in a wheelchair before, and it seemed strange. But he was glad to see that Gramps was not wearing his pajamas. Instead, Gramps had dressed for the occasion in his favorite corduroy pants and green-checkered shirt.

"You made it, Mars Bars!" Gramps cried happily as Marty and Russell entered the room. Marty put Measle's cage on the bed and then rushed over to give Gramps a hug.

"And how are the special agents doing?" Gramps asked, looking at Russell.

"They're fine, except that Charlie's turning into a chewing machine," Russell said with a grin. "When he's loose in my bedroom, he takes little nibbles of everything—my blanket, my pillow, even the socks under my bed."

"And they've probably been under there for weeks." Gramps laughed.

"More like months," Russell said sheepishly.

"The mouse's taste buds must be shot by now. And what about you, Mars Bars?" Gramps asked. "What have you been up to?"

Suddenly Marty remembered the letters. He pulled off his backpack and reached inside.

"He wrote back, Gramps," Marty said, handing his grandfather the long gray envelope. "Napoleon really wrote back."

With trembling hands, Gramps opened the envelope and unfolded the letter. He pulled his thick black reading glasses out of his pocket and slowly began to read the fancy black script.

"Why, that old coot," Gramps muttered with a shake of his head.

"Who, Napoleon?" Marty asked with surprise.

"No, not Napoleon, Henry Cooper," Gramps said, looking up from the letter. "That old coot, Henry Cooper, did it! He really got your letter through!" Gramps's dark brown eyes were large and twinkling behind the thick glasses.

"Don't forget the bet," Russell whispered, tugging on Marty's sleeve.

"Oh yeah, Gramps, there's something else," Marty said, reaching into his backpack and pulling out his letter to Abraham Lincoln. "Do you think Cooper's Secret Courier Service could mail another letter?" He handed Gramps the envelope.

"To President Abraham Lincoln, Washington, D.C.," Gramps read aloud. He looked at the boys and grinned. "Why not?" he whispered.

"Whew." Russell sighed as Gramps tucked the letter into his shirt pocket.

"Now both of you boys must understand that this has to be top-secret stuff." Gramps's face had suddenly turned serious. "If your mother or any of the nurses were to hear about Henry Cooper's Secret Courier Service, they'd think we were batty. They wouldn't believe it, and they'd probably come up with some kind of medication to make us stop having hallucinations." He waved Napoleon's letter in the air. "Some hallucination, hey, Mars Bars!" Suddenly a nurse's voice drifted in from the hallway. Gramps quickly handed the letter back to Marty, then brought his index finger to his lips. "Mum's the word," he said softly.

"Mum's the word," Marty and Russell both whispered, bringing their fingers up to their lips.

"So what do you think of my new wheels?" Gramps asked, patting the arm of his chair.

"Cool," Marty said. "But what does it sing?"

Gramps laughed. "It's not as musical as the beast, but this baby has speed. Want to see?"

"Sure," Marty replied as he and Russell backed away from the wheelchair. Gramps headed for the door, but before he could get out, Mrs. Bellucci rushed into the room.

"So much for racing," Marty whispered to Russ as he watched his mother hovering over Gramps.

"What about the mailroom?" Russ whispered back. "Do you think we'll get to see it today?"

"I hope so, but we'll have to wait," Marty told him.

"Oh, Pop, you look great today," Mrs. Bellucci said to Gramps. She swooped down and gave him a big kiss, leaving a bright red lipstick mouth on his cheek. Marty couldn't help but notice how pale Gramps's face looked next to the bright red mark.

"The nurses said that we're all to report to the recreation room for Pet Day," Mrs. Bellucci told the boys. "Mrs. Furness, the social director, has her office there, and everyone who is bringing a pet must check in with her."

"I'll lead the way," Gramps said, wheeling his chair across the room. He leaned over and picked up Measle's cage, placing it on his lap. Neither Measle nor Charlie had ever ridden in a wheelchair before. Marty was glad they were getting the chance. He wanted his mouse to experience as much of the world as he could. Out in the hall, Gramps said hello to everyone he passed.

"This is my grandson Mars Bars and his friend Russell the Muscle," he said to anyone who would listen. He stuck his head in room 226 and called, "Hey, Johnson, I've got my wheels revved up. How about burning a little rubber?"

"Give it up, Picardi," an old man answered. "I'm watching my shows—now, don't bother me."

"He's a little cranky in the morning," Gramps said, scratching his head. "And a little crabby in the afternoon. Come to think of it, the early evening's not much better." Gramps cracked his crooked smile. "Actually, you could say that old Johnson's a little crabby right up until the sun goes down."

"Maybe he's a vampire," Marty suggested. This was all Gramps needed to hear.

"You know, Mars Bars, you're probably right. I can't tell you the number of people I've seen around this place who looked like somebody had sucked the blood right out of them."

"Maybe we could try and catch him," Marty suggested with a giggle.

"Who?" Mrs. Bellucci wanted to know.

"The vampire," Russell told her.

But Gramps was shaking his head. "It's a tricky business trying to catch a vampire. They disguise themselves so well. Now, this vampire could be anyone here." Gramps held his hand over his neck as a pretty young nurse walked by. "It could be anybody," he whispered. "Even though it would have to be a very old vampire, it could take on the shape of a younger person." He had a worried look on his face as he surveyed the length of the hall.

"Why would it have to be an old vampire?" Russell whispered back.

Gramps's eyebrows shot up. "Are you kidding? After sucking up all this old blood, the thing would have to be ancient."

"Enough! Enough!" Marty's mother cried. "Marty, why did you have to get him started? And Pop, you know I've asked you a hundred times not to be filling Marty with such crazy ideas. He and Russell will probably have nightmares all night now."

"We won't, we won't!" Marty and Russell sang together. They both wanted to hear more about the old bloodsucking vampire. But Mrs. Bellucci put her foot down.

"If they won't have nightmares, then I will, so please stop," she insisted. Gramps shrugged as Marty and Russell sighed with disappointment.

"Oh, look," Mrs. Bellucci said, pointing to the recreation room. "There go some people with their pets. They must be here for Pet Day too."

Marty and Russell followed Gramps and Mrs. Bellucci into a large room with a red line painted down the middle. There was a Ping-Pong table in one corner and a television set in another. A group of old people were sitting on a couch and in wheelchairs around an oval coffee table. Several children carrying boxes and assorted pet carriers stood beside them. A chubby redheaded woman of about forty was in the center of the group. This was Mrs. Furness, the social director.

"Hello, Mr. Picardi," she said cheerfully as Gramps wheeled his chair to the edge of the circle. "I see that your family has arrived." Gramps nodded.

"Please, everyone take a seat and we'll begin with our main visit, before going on to individual rooms later for those residents who are unable to leave their beds." Marty looked at Gramps. He was glad that he was well enough to leave his bed. With his clothes on, Gramps looked almost well enough to go home.

Marty made a secret wish, then and there. He wished that Gramps would feel so good that by the end of the day he wouldn't need the wheelchair at all, and they could pack up his things and take him home.

"This is Mr. Sipes and his granddaughter Becky," Marty heard Mrs. Furness saying. He looked up to see an old bald-headed man sitting in a wheelchair, with a bright multicolored blanket over his knees. Mr. Sipes had the biggest, bumpiest nose that Marty had ever seen. His head had rolled to one side, and he seemed to have fallen asleep.

To Marty and Russell's great delight, the old man suddenly began to snore. The noise grew louder and louder. The snores were great gargly snores that echoed off the walls and bounced off the carpet. Marty couldn't decide whether Mr. Sipes sounded like a whale, a bear, or a big old cement truck. He finally decided that he sounded like all three. Marty closed his eyes and in his mind saw a great lumbering whale with a bear's face, only instead of eyes, the bear face had headlights, and instead of fins, the whale had wheels, and instead of spraying air out of his blowhole, the whale sprayed cement!

Marty sat with his eyes closed, listening intently to the wondrous snores and letting his imagination run wild. Suddenly, the snoring came to an abrupt stop. Marty opened his eyes and saw Mrs. Furness gently shaking Mr. Sipes by the shoulder.

Becky Sipes was standing by his wheelchair,

looking mortified. She was about twelve or thirteen years old, Marty guessed, though he couldn't figure out why she looked so unhappy. Marty loved to hear Gramps snore, though Gramps was a lightweight compared to Mr. Sipes. Mr. Sipes was a contender for the world's greatest snorer.

"That's a remarkable pet you've got there, Becky," Mrs. Furness said. Marty and Russell had been so absorbed by the remarkable snores, they hadn't even looked at the small glass aquarium that sat on the oval table beside Becky Sipes. Looking at it now, they nudged each other excitedly.

"Oh, cool, a snake," Russell whispered as they watched Becky shyly tap on the aquarium. The snake uncoiled itself and stretched up alongside the glass.

"Becky lives in Washington, D.C.," Mrs. Furness said.

"She's going to be a member of Congress someday. Isn't that right, honey?" Mr. Sipes added. But Becky didn't answer. She seemed embarrassed.

"Where did she get the snake? At the White

House?" Russell asked. Everyone except Becky laughed at this. Her grandfather seemed to laugh the loudest.

"They may have a snake or two at the White House, besides the usual pests." Mr. Sipes winked at Gramps and chuckled. Marty was confused. He wondered if Mr. Sipes meant that the president was a snake or a pest.

"Mr. Sipes was an exterminator for many years," Mrs. Furness told the group. "He retired after Becky's father took over the business. Mr. Sipes even worked at the White House once, isn't that true, George?"

"That's the truth." Mr. Sipes smiled proudly. "A top-security job, though. Those cockroaches in the White House were no different from the cockroaches we'd find in the poorest buildings. Bugs are bugs, you know."

Marty and Russell sat staring at Becky Sipes. She not only had a snake, but she also had a grandfather who could easily be in *The Guinness Book of World Records* for the most amazing snores, and if this weren't enough, he had also killed cockroaches in the White House!

Mrs. Furness asked Becky to tell the group

a little something about her pet. Becky explained that she had found the snake in the woods behind her grandparents' house, and that before she returned to Washington on this trip, she would let it go.

Mrs. Furness suggested that Becky walk around the group with her aquarium, so that everyone could get a closer look at her pet. Marty and Russell leaned over in their seats, hoping to study the snake's markings, but the girl seemed too embarrassed to stand in front of them for more than a few seconds.

"Does anyone have any questions for Becky?" Mrs. Furness asked. Everyone could see how uncomfortable Becky looked, so no one asked her anything, although Marty was dying to ask her if she could snore as loudly as her grandfather.

"Thank you, Becky, and next we have Miss Lucy Hillvaney's great-niece, Little Lucy," Mrs. Furness said, pointing to a golden-haired girl of about seven. The girl was leaning on the wheelchair of an old shriveled-up woman. Miss Hillvaney's silver wig had slipped down over her left eye. Suddenly Marty realized that he had seen this woman before. It was the same old woman that he and his mother had spoken to on their last visit, the same old woman that he had dreamed about.

"Little Lucy came this weekend all the way from New Jersey," Mrs. Furness told the group. "And can you tell us a little something about your pet? Or should I say pets?"

Little Lucy smiled proudly. Her two front teeth were missing, and she kept swishing her tongue back and forth, trying to fill in the empty spaces.

"These are my ants, and they live in this ant farm," she said, holding up a thin plastic box. Marty had a hard time seeing any of the ants. "You can't touch them because they bite."

"Lucy, I can see the family resemblance," an old woman said, staring up from the couch. She was speaking to the old Lucy, who smiled and nodded.

"She's the spitting image of me back when I was a girl," Miss Hillvaney said in a dry, crackly sort of whisper. "I have a picture that my father took of our family in 1911. This little one looks so much like me, you'd think she stepped out of that picture."

Marty stared at the old woman and then at the little girl. Spitting image? Family resemblance? What were they talking about? The little girl was full of life, with her smooth skin and her golden blond curls, while the old woman was a shriveled bent figure, looking more like a scarecrow than a person. It seemed impossible that someone so old could have ever looked young.

Little Lucy went on to tell the group about her ants, how she had to send away for them and how they were much bigger than ordinary house ants, and how some of them had died. Actually, most of them had died and at the last count she was down to three.

"This one is Roxanne, this one is Tara, and this one is Melissa," she said, pointing to each one.

"What dumb names for ants," Marty whispered. Russell nodded in agreement, but he still listened attentively to all Little Lucy had to say, since he was hoping to get an ant farm himself on his next birthday.

Little Lucy then walked around the circle, giving everyone a chance to look at her "babies."

"When I was a girl, I wasn't allowed to have a pet," the old Lucy said. "We had ten children in our family, and I was the oldest. I was always helping my mother with the babies. My father didn't believe in children having pets. He said that it was wasteful to feed an animal that we weren't going to eat.

"My father was raising pigs then, and one day I woke up to find that eight new piglets had been born. One of them seemed smaller and daintier than the rest. I called her Angel, and I always managed to save a little piece of my dinner and sneak it out to her in the barn. I really loved that little pig. She had the bluest eyes you ever saw.

"Well, of course, with all the extra food, Angel grew fatter and fatter, and before I realized what I'd done, my father was bragging that he had the fattest pig in the county. When he sold her at the fair, I cried myself to sleep every night, feeling so guilty. My mother asked me why I was crying, and I told her that I had killed Angel by making her so fat. I told her I wished I had been taking food out of her trough instead of putting it in, and then maybe she wouldn't have been sold. Mother just laughed and said that fat or skinny, Angel was a pig and pigs are grown to be eaten. We raised a lot of pigs after that, though I never snuck food out of the house to any of them, and you know, none were ever as fat or as beautiful as my Angel."

Mrs. Furness smiled and reached over to adjust Miss Hillvaney's slipping wig. Marty suddenly felt sorry for the old Lucy. He knew how sad she must have been when Angel got sold. He looked down at Measle and was glad that he was a mouse and not a pig. When he looked up again, he found himself staring at the two Lucys. Now he could see a resemblance between the old woman and the little girl. It was something about the shape of their faces and the soft blue-gray color of their eyes.

There were a number of children who showed their pets after Little Lucy. Mr. Grossman's granddaughter had a parakeet. Mr. Curry's grandson had a turtle, and Mrs. Barta's grandson had a hamster. But what really surprised Marty were the stories about the interesting lives that the old people had led. They had worked at all kinds of jobs.

Mr. Curry had been an electrician and had worked on the roller coaster at Coney Island. Mrs. Barta was born in France and had been a dancer and a puppeteer in Europe. She told the group about the puppet show she had once put on for the cousin of the Queen of England.

"I have family still living in Paris. They have a little theater," she told the group.

Mr. Grossman had been a baker. He told them about the mouse that had climbed into one of his batter bowls and had almost been baked into a jelly doughnut before it was rescued. Everyone seemed to have a story to tell about work and friends and family.

"Mr. Picardi, would you like to introduce your grandson and his friend?" Mrs. Furness finally said. Marty's mouth felt dry at the thought of having to speak in front of everyone. He nervously stood up and walked beside Russell to the center of the circle. Gramps proudly wheeled his chair between the two.

"This is my grandson," Gramps said, reach-

ing out for Marty's sleeve. "Martin 'Mars Bars'
Bellucci and his sidekick Russell the Muscle.
Now, if there are any vampires in the audience, I'm warning you, you don't want to mess
with these two."

Chapter 12

Mrs. Bellucci rolled her eyes and Marty and Russell giggled. Gramps continued, "They have brought their two pets to show you today. Now, I know you've all seen mice before, but these two are something special, nothing ordinary about them, no sirree, they're not like other mice at all. Marty, why don't you tell the folks a little something about them?"

Marty held up the cage for everyone to see. "Uh, this is Measle. He's the one with the spot on his back." He pointed to Measle. "His best friend is Charlie, who belongs to my best friend, Russ."

As Russell began to tell the group about Charlie and his bad habit of chewing anything in sight, Mr. Curry leaned forward in his wheelchair. The old man's face turned bright red as he began to cough. The veins along the side of his head were blue and bulging while he gasped for air.

A nurse ordered an aide to "get the oxygen." The aide ran to the end of the room and wheeled an oxygen tank over to Mr. Curry's wheelchair. While the aide placed a mask over Mr. Curry's face, the nurse pressed her stethoscope to his chest and opened his shirt. Everyone grew quiet as she listened to his heart.

"Let's get him back to his room," she finally said. Mr. Curry was quickly wheeled out of the room, along with the oxygen tank. Meanwhile, Mr. Curry's daughter-in-law turned and looked at her son, who had placed his turtle back in its box.

"David, I've got to go with Grandpa. I'll be right back," she whispered.

"Don't worry, we'll look after him," Mrs. Bellucci assured her, placing her arm around the boy. Marty looked at David Curry, who stood biting down on his lower lip, trying not to cry.

"I want to go with my mom and Grandpa," he whimpered.

"The nurses are taking care of your grandfather now," Mrs. Bellucci told him. She looked at Gramps. "Pop, is there a place we can get him a soda?"

Gramps turned his wheelchair toward the door. "There's a soda machine in the dining room." As Marty picked up Measle's cage and began to follow them, his mother shook her head.

"I don't think they'd appreciate mice in the dining room, Marty. You and Russell can wait here with the pets. Gramps, David, and I will be right back."

It was very quiet in the recreation room. No one was smiling anymore, and some of the people got up to leave. Marty and Russell walked over to the turtle, wondering whether it would be all right to take it out of the box. Mrs. Furness suggested they sit on some folding chairs outside her office.

"You can take your mice, but we'll leave David's turtle on the table," she said. They watched as she turned on the television set, as if to try to dispel the sudden cloud of gloom that hung over the room. A few more residents walked or wheeled themselves back to their rooms, while the rest stared sullenly ahead as a game-show announcer on the television barked, "Big money! We're looking for some big money!"

No one seemed to care about the TV show or the "big money." They're probably all thinking about Mr. Curry, thought Marty. He felt sorry for David Curry, but he also was envious that he was getting a soda. Marty looked up to see Mrs. Furness walking toward them.

"I'm sure the nurses will help Mr. Curry. He's had these spells before," she said. "I have a few phone calls to make, but if you need me, come right in." She smiled before disappearing into her office.

Marty and Russell looked down at Measle and Charlie, in the cage on the floor in front of them. Measle was running circles around Charlie. As the two boys gazed at the mice, a blond-haired boy of about seven or eight walked into the recreation room. He was carrying a large white box. He seemed to know exactly where he was going. He briskly walked toward Mrs. Furness's office, looking neither to his left nor right. As the boy walked past them into the office, Marty read the words KITTY CARRIER across the side of the box.

"Please take a seat outside, and I'll be right with you," Marty heard Mrs. Furness say. Within seconds, the boy came out of the office and sat down beside Marty, placing the Kitty Carrier next to Measle's cage.

Marty stared at the Kitty Kid. (When Marty saw someone that he didn't know, he sometimes made up a name for him. The Kitty Kid was the name he was thinking of when the boy sat next to him.)

Marty looked down at Measle and Charlie and frowned. They wouldn't be very comfortable with a Kitty Carrier sitting beside them. Marty was wondering if he should move the cage, when he caught a whiff of something new in the air. Something good. It smelled like candy. He looked up to see the Kitty Kid open a bag and pull out a long stick of ruby red licorice. Marty guessed that there were at least ten more sticks in the bag.

Red licorice was one of Marty's favorite candies. Gramps used to buy it for him when they went to a movie. Marty closed his eyes, inhaling the wonderful sweet licorice scent.

"That's the best thing I've smelled so far today," Marty said loudly. He was hoping the Kitty Kid would offer him a piece of candy, but the boy ignored his remark. It looked like he was going to eat the entire bag of candy himself.

Suddenly a loud "meow" came from the Kitty Carrier. Then more meows. They grew threatening as they were accompanied by a loud scratching noise against the sides of the box. Marty and Russell looked down and saw Measle and Charlie huddled in a corner of their cage.

"I wonder how big his 'kitty' is?" Russell whispered to Marty. The Kitty Kid grinned.

"Big enough to eat your two little rats in one swallow," he said with a sneer.

"They aren't rats," Russell snapped back.

"They're mice," Marty said, bringing his sneaker close to the cage.

"Rats, mice, what's the difference? Crusher could swallow them whole," the boy replied.

"Crusher?" Marty and Russell repeated the name nervously.

"Yeah, he's the kind of cat that likes to crush things. He's a killer cat when it comes to rats." The Kitty Kid's grin was not unlike that of Mr. Bullner. Marty wanted to pick up Measle's cage, but he didn't want the boy to see that he was worried. He looked at the Kitty Carrier.

How big could this Crusher be? he wondered. From the sound of his meows, he was probably big. Could he be filling up the entire box? And how sharp were his teeth? What about his claws? Marty cringed as he heard them scratching against the sides of the box. They sounded long, sharp, and deadly.

Marty gazed at Measle, who blinked up at him, a fluffy little clump of white fur.

"Yeah, they sure are wimpy-looking things," the boy said with a shake of his head. Marty's cheeks grew hot. Was he going to let this Kitty Kid person get away with calling his mouse a wimp?

"These aren't ordinary mice," Marty said quickly.

"Oh no?" The boy cocked his head.

"No," Marty replied, remembering

Gramps's words. "They're not like other mice at all."

"So what kind of mice are they?" the boy asked.

"Go on, Marty," Russell said confidently. "Tell him what kind of mice they are." Sweat gathered on Marty's upper lip. He had no idea what kind of mice they were. Why did he ever say they weren't ordinary? He and Russell both knew that Measle and Charlie were the most ordinary mice in the world.

"So?" the boy asked.

Chapter 13

The Kitty Kid tapped on the top of the cage with his stick of licorice. Marty squirmed in his seat. He kicked the leg of his chair. He knew he had to say something, but what? Suddenly the faintest hint of a smile crept onto Marty's face. He looked down at Measle and Charlie and then, with a dramatic sweep of his head, turned toward the boy.

"These aren't ordinary mice," Marty cautioned. "These mice are experimental."

"Experimental?" the Kitty Kid asked.

Marty looked around the room again, then leaned closer to the boy. "My dad works for NASA. My parents are divorced, and my dad is living in Florida." He shot a look at Russell, whose eyes had become as big as silver dollars. Marty decided he better not overdo it.

"My dad's not an astronaut or anything," he continued. "He works in space research. Anyway, NASA needed a home for these mice after they returned to Earth on a space shuttle."

"Yeah, right," the boy groaned.

"Haven't you ever heard of animals being sent into space?" Marty asked.

"Where? Where did the space shuttle go?" the Kitty Kid asked.

"Out of this solar system," Marty answered. His voice was low, steady, and completely convincing. "They were the only living things on the shuttle. They were traveling so fast and so far, they were . . . well, changed."

"How did they change?" Russell asked. Marty shot him a disapproving look. "I . . . I . . . mean, tell him how they changed," Russell quickly added. "Of course I know how they changed. Boy, did they change!"

"I don't know if I should tell anyone else," Marty said. "It's supposed to be top secret. I already told Russ here, and I have to be careful. NASA doesn't want the information leaking to the newspapers or TV."

"I won't tell anyone," the boy assured him.

Marty sat farther back in his seat, silently staring at the bag of licorice.

The Kitty Kid reached inside. "Here, you can each have a piece," he said, offering a stick to Marty and then to Russell. A loud "meow" came from the box as Marty sank his teeth into the soft red candy.

"Okay, I guess I can tell you," said Marty, swallowing a big bite. "But you have to promise never to repeat what I'm about to say."

The boy nodded. "I promise. I promise," he answered. Marty stuffed the rest of the licorice stick in his mouth and stared at the bag.

"Oh, here, have another piece," the Kitty Kid said. "Now, go on, tell me. How did they change?"

"Their molecules changed," Marty told him. "It's a complicated thing that happens in space travel. Has to do with space particles and light." He spoke with all the seriousness of a NASA researcher as he stuffed the other licorice stick into his mouth. "But to put it as simply as I can . . ." He leaned over and took a third stick of licorice from the bag without asking. The boy didn't stop him, although

when Russell tried to do the same thing, the
Kitty Kid pulled the bag away and Russell almost fell off his chair.

"So how are they changed? With their molecules and stuff?" the boy asked. Marty hesi-
tated a few seconds to build suspense, the way
Gramps often did when telling a story.

"To put it simply," he said, "these mice can
fly!"

The boy's mouth dropped open. Russell's
eyes rolled up to the ceiling. Marty silently
reached for the licorice bag and held it in his
hand. The boy was so busy looking in Measle's
cage, he didn't seem to care about his candy
anymore.

"But they don't have wings. How can they
fly if they don't have wings?" he wanted to
know.

Marty chewed on another stick of licorice.
"They aren't like ordinary flying things," he
decided. "I told you, they're not ordinary. The
wings sprout from under their fur when . . .
when their temperature goes up. It has to do
with body heat. When they get excited, they
undergo a—a molecular transformation."

Marty wasn't sure what a molecular transformation was. Once he had heard a mad scientist talk about it on a Frankenstein cartoon. Ever since, he had wanted to mention it in conversation.

Russell gave Marty the thumbs-up signal as the Kitty Kid continued to stare at Measle and Charlie. "Show me," he demanded. "If they can really fly, let's see them do it."

Russell looked at Marty and frowned. Marty looked at Measle and Charlie and frowned.

"I told you it has to do with body heat. They only sprout their wings when they get excited and have energy. They need their sleep now," he explained. "I don't want to wake them up." All three boys looked down at the cage. Measle and Charlie looked back with dark brown eyes.

"They aren't sleeping. And they aren't space mice," the boy declared, grabbing the half-empty bag of candy from Marty's hands.

"Well, they may not be sleeping, but they're resting," Marty replied. "They did so much flying around my bedroom this morning, they need to rest. It's too bad you weren't there.

You could have seen them fly up to my ceiling. They're really tired out now."

The boy sat silently for a few minutes, staring at his Kitty Carrier.

"I know something that can wake them up," he whispered, bending over the box. "Something that can really get them excited."

Before either Marty or Russell could stop him, the Kitty Kid opened the carrier and lifted out Crusher, the killer cat of rats.

Chapter 14

"That's Crusher?" Marty and Russell gasped as they looked at a fluffy little calico kitten.

"But he's only a kitten!" Marty said, staring at the soft ball of orange and brown fur. Crusher yawned and rubbed his dainty head against the boy's chest.

"He may be only a kitten now," the boy explained, "but when he starts to grow, he's going to be huge."

Russell and Marty exchanged looks, relieved to see that Crusher was not as threatening as they once thought.

But to Measle and Charlie, things looked quite different. While the Kitty Kid held the kitten next to the cage, the two mice took one look at Crusher's long kitten whiskers and his big gray kitten eyes and scampered to the back of the cage. Then they started running from side to side.

"Boy, they really are excited." The boy giggled, still holding Crusher in front of them. "They should be sprouting wings anytime now."

"Hey, cut that out," Marty said, picking up the cage and trying to hold it away from the kitten. But by this time, Measle and Charlie were in such a state of panic, they couldn't sit still. With a surge of energy, the two crashed against the cage door, breaking the string latch that Charlie had been nibbling on in the car. The door flew open, and Measle and Charlie fell to the carpeted floor, scurrying across the room as fast as their little feet could carry them.

Crusher took one look at the mice and quickly wiggled out of the boy's grip, racing across the floor after them. The old people in the room were all shouting and calling after the escaped animals. Marty and Russell leaped up from their chairs. The pets had already scampered out the door, into the hall.

"Are they flying yet?" the Kitty Kid shouted, running after them. Soon the doorway was crowded with wheelchairs and walkers, since a number of old people had come to join the search. Marty and Russell looked up and down the corridor, but there was no sign of the runaway animals.

"Where did they go?" Russell cried as he and Marty stared at the dozens of open doorways leading off the hallway.

"Don't worry, we'll help you find them," Mrs. Barta said, coming up beside them.

"We'll turn this place upside down if we have to," Mr. Sipes added from his wheelchair.

"The baby is taking a nap, so now would be a good time to look." Miss Hillvaney shook her head.

"What baby?" Russell whispered to Marty.

"Oh, she gets confused," Marty told him as they peeked into the doorway of an open room. "I'll explain later." Soon the hallway was full of residents walking and wheeling in and out of rooms, calling, "Here, kitty, kitty," and "Here, Measle. Come on, Charlie." The little group from the recreation room had swelled to quite a number as more and more old people joined in the hunt.

"Here, Measle. Here, Charlie. Come on, Crusher." The calls grew louder and louder as new voices picked up the chant.

"This is more fun than bingo!" an old man cackled.

"What is going on here?" Mrs. Furness gasped, stepping into the hall.

"Shh, shh. We're trying to find the animals before the baby wakes up," Miss Hillvaney whispered.

"What animals? Oh no!" said Mrs. Furness as she caught a glimpse of the empty cage in Marty's hand. "You don't mean to tell me that they're loose?" she cried. Before Marty or Russell could reply, the Kitty Kid spoke up.

"Don't worry, Mrs. Furness." He grinned. "My cat, Crusher, is out looking for them right now. He can take care of those wimpy mice."

"The cat is loose too!" she cried. "How did this happen?" Marty's cheeks burned with embarrassment.

"Oh no, what will I tell Miss Ruddles?" Mrs.

Furness moaned as she looked down the hall. A thin woman in a navy suit was dodging wheelchairs and walkers as she hurried toward them. It was Miss Ruddles, the director of Shady Maples, and she did not look happy.

"Mrs. Furness, will you please tell me what in heaven's name is going on here?" Miss Ruddles demanded in a screechy voice.

"They're loose! They're all loose!" Mrs. Barta cried as she wheeled by.

"Who's loose?" Miss Ruddles wanted to know.

"The animals," Mr. Sipes said. "But don't you worry about it, Miss Ruddles, because you've got an expert here to take care of things. Why, I've caught more mice in my time than—"

"Mice! Did you say mice!" Miss Ruddles screeched.

"It's okay, they're trained," Russell told her, "except for Charlie and his chewing thing. . . ." His voice trailed off as he saw the pained look on Miss Ruddles's face.

"Never in all my years at Shady Maples has anything like this ever happened!" she fumed.

"Mrs. Furness, this Pet Day was your project and your responsibility, and I'd like you to explain how such a thing could have happened!" Her thin, pinched face turned a bright crimson, her mouth twitched, and her eyes glared at Mrs. Furness.

Mrs. Furness was trembling and looked like she was about to cry. Just then, the Kitty Kid stepped forward.

"It's not her fault!" he shouted. "It's his." He pointed to Marty. "He told me that his mice could fly."

A hush came over the hallway as everyone looked at Marty. Even Russell stared at him. Marty took a little step backward and tried to smile.

"Flying mice; that's pretty funny," he mumbled. "Whoever heard of flying mice?"

Chapter 15

"Martin Bellucci, how could you tell such a lie?" Marty's mother demanded as she hurried into the recreation room. Miss Ruddles had ordered the boys to wait there while the residents were settled back in their rooms and the custodians were alerted to the animals' escape. Mrs. Furness had told Mrs. Bellucci the entire story.

"I am so sorry about all this," Mrs. Bellucci said, turning to the frazzled-looking Mrs. Furness. "I'm afraid that Marty's always had an overactive imagination."

"I don't want to imagine what Miss Ruddles will do if we can't find those mice by the end of the day. She's a stickler for order, you know," Mrs. Furness said. "I'd better see how the search is going."

"We can help you," Marty offered. Russell and the Kitty Kid nodded.

"No!" Mrs. Furness cried. "I mean, no thank you, boys," she said, trying to compose herself. "I think it best that you stay here for now." She turned and walked into the hall.

"Where's Gramps?" Marty whispered to his mother.

"He's still with David in the dining room," Mrs. Bellucci replied. "Marty, I'm surprised at you for telling such a story. Just look at the commotion you've caused."

"It didn't seem like such a big deal at the time," Marty answered. "I guess I got a little carried away."

"A little carried away? Flying mice? You're getting as bad as Gramps." Mrs. Bellucci groaned. "And poor Mrs. Furness. I'd better go see if there is anything I can do. You two stay here. I'll be right back."

Marty watched as she walked out of the room.

"Poor Mrs. Furness? I'd say it's more like poor Charlie and Measle. I wonder where they are?" Russell said.

"I hope they don't have traps set," Marty mused, looking under the pool table.

"Or poison," Russell muttered.

"If they've put poison out, Crusher will eat it. He eats just about anything," the Kitty Kid said anxiously. "Can a cat die from eating mouse poison?"

"People can die from eating mouse poison, so I guess cats can too," Russell told him.

The Kitty Kid suddenly burst into tears. "I don't want Crusher to die. I don't want him to die," he sobbed.

"Don't worry," Russell said, putting his arm around him. "They'll find him soon."

"But what if he's eating the poison right now?" the Kitty Kid whimpered.

Marty jumped to his feet. "I can't sit here while Measle could be eating poison," he declared. "No one knows our pets like we do. If anyone is going to find them, it's going to be us."

"But Marty," Russell cried, "what about your mom and Mrs. Furness? They told us to wait here, remember?"

Marty walked toward the door. "I know,

Russ, but I don't think they thought of the poison. If my mom knew that Measle could be eating poison, she'd want me to do everything I could to try and save him." He stuck his head through the doorway and peeked down the hall. Russell and the Kitty Kid followed close behind.

"Come on," Marty whispered. "Let's go." He led the way, running to the first open door. It was Miss Hillvaney's room. Little Lucy was sitting in a chair, watching Roxanne, Melissa, and Tara tunnel through a hill while Old Lucy was lying in bed. Her flowery dress was pulled up around her bony knees. Lucy's mother was washing Miss Hillvaney's feet.

"Excuse me," said Marty. "We're just looking for . . ."

"Oh, that's quite all right." Old Lucy smiled from her bed. "But you know, we searched the room already."

"I hope you find them," Little Lucy said, placing her arm around her ant farm.

"Thank you," said the boys, stepping out the door.

Marty scanned the hallway and decided that

with so many open doors, it would be better if
they split up.

"Russ, you check the rooms across the hall,
and I'll look in the rooms on this side," he
ordered.

"Right," Russ answered. He quickly crossed
the hall and ducked into an empty room.

"What about me?" the Kitty Kid wanted to
know. "Where should I look?" Marty frowned.
It's going to be hard enough sneaking into
rooms without a little kid tagging along, he
thought.

"Maybe you should wait in the recreation
room," he suggested. The Kitty Kid frowned.

"Listen to me," Marty began again. "Cats are
great backtrackers. I heard of a cat who got lost
and then backtracked his way across the coun-
try to find his owner. Cats think of their owners as their parents, you know. And they miss
them just like you'd miss your mom or dad.
Measle and Charlie are mice, and they're different. Mice are natural explorers, but
Crusher is a backtracker. It's in a cat's blood.
I bet he's waiting back there for you right now,
wondering where you are."

The Kitty Kid stood thinking this over. "Okay," he said, "but if you find him first, you'll come and get me, won't you?"

"Sure." Marty smiled as the Kitty Kid headed down the hall.

Marty stepped through an open doorway. It was a large closet of some kind. He switched on the light and quickly shut the door.

"Here, Measle. Here, Charlie," Marty began to call softly. The walls were lined with shelves stacked with folded white sheets and towels.

"Are you guys hiding back here?" Marty whispered. He put Measle's empty cage on a shelf and began searching behind the stacks of linen. "Come on, Measle, you can come out now." His hand stopped as it came across something hard and round. Marty dropped some towels on the floor and stood staring at an old glass doorknob. He pulled a few more stacks of towels off the shelves.

"It's a door!" Marty exclaimed. Then he climbed up onto a stepladder, pushed some more sheets to one side, and discovered two faded, cracked letters in the center of the old oak door. They were painted in gold.

"M. R." Marty read the letters aloud. "M. R., what could that stand for?" Suddenly it came to him. "M.R. must stand for Mail Room! This must be a secret door! The secret door to Henry Cooper's mailroom!" He quickly climbed down the stepladder and began searching along the sides of the shelves for a button or lever.

There must be some way to move these shelves back, Marty thought, as he heard a knock on the closet door. He threw the towels back on the shelves, picked up the cage, and took a step toward the door. The second knock was louder.

"Who is it?" Marty whispered.

"It's me, Walter," came a little voice.

"Walter?"

"You know, Crusher's father."

Marty opened the closet door and stuck out his head. The Kitty Kid stood grinning before him.

"Look who backtracked!" the Kitty Kid cried, glancing down at his shirt pocket where two little white heads were poking out.

"Measle! Charlie!" Marty scooped up the two trembling mice. "How did you catch them?" he asked, cuddling Measle to his cheek before putting the two mice in their cage.

"These are the first mice I ever caught," the Kitty Kid announced. "When I saw them, I put down a piece of licorice. They came over, and this one started chewing on it right away."

"That's Charlie, all right," Marty laughed. The Kitty Kid laughed too. But their laughter was suddenly interrupted.

"What are you doing in there? Come out this instant!" It was Miss Ruddles. She had her hand on the doorknob, and when she pulled it toward her, Marty fell out of the closet onto the Kitty Kid. The cage tumbled to the floor and Charlie sprang out. The frightened mouse scurried in circles around Marty's feet and raced onto Miss Ruddles's shoe!

"Agh! A mouse! A mouse!" Miss Ruddles screamed. Little Lucy came running out of Miss Hillvaney's room to see what was going on. Miss Ruddles threw herself back and crashed into Little Lucy, who was still holding her ants. The ant farm was flipped into the air

and landed on the floor with such force that
the top fell off.

With Roxanne in the lead, the three ants
took off down the hall, skittering from right to
left.

Little Lucy let out a piercing wail that could
be heard in every corner of Shady Maples. It
even woke up Mr. Sipes, who was mid-snore
in his nap.

"What's all the noise about? Can't take a
nap in this place without getting woken up
by a bunch of screaming meemies. Are you
trying to give me cardiac arrest? Good grief!"
he exclaimed as he came barreling out of his
room in his wheelchair. He promptly col-
lided with Miss Ruddles, who landed on the
floor. Charlie looked as if he were about to
take a nibble out of her shoe, when Mr.
Sipes threw down the blanket that was covering his knees. It was a direct hit, covering
Charlie completely.

Marty knelt, trying to follow the little bump
that was moving beneath the brightly colored
blanket. He reached underneath and pulled
Charlie into the open while Miss Ruddles

leaped to her feet. (Miss Ruddles was not the kind of person who wanted people to see her sitting on the floor.)

The Kitty Kid held the cage so that Marty could put Charlie back inside beside Measle. Marty held the door shut while the Kitty Kid reached in his pocket and pulled out a little piece of plastic-coated wire. He said he always saved the wire ties that his mother tied around his sandwich bags at lunch. He handed it to Marty, who carefully wired the door shut.

"Good work," Mr. Sipes said.

"Thanks," Marty replied. "I hope this will hold better than the string. And thanks for helping me catch Charlie."

"Mouse catching is in my blood," Mr. Sipes said as he leaned over from his wheelchair and picked up his blanket. "But catching ants, that's a different story. We aren't in the habit of taking prisoners, if you know what I mean." Marty looked down the hall at Little Lucy, who was trying to catch her babies. Most of the residents had come out of their rooms and were searching for the lost ants.

"Here, Roxanne. Here, Melissa. Here, Tara," Little Lucy called.

"Don't worry," Becky Sipes said. "We've got plenty of ants in our kitchen back home. Maybe I can mail you a few."

Chapter 16

"It's probably a good thing that no one found those ants," the Kitty Kid said later as he and Marty followed Miss Ruddles back to the recreation room. "They aren't like regular ants—they're bigger and they bite."

Miss Ruddles frowned. "Now we'll have to hire an exterminator to come in and fumigate the entire building," she said, glaring at Mrs. Furness. Just then, Russell came running through the doorway. A number of old people walked or wheeled in behind him.

"Look, Russ, we found them," Marty called, holding up Measle's cage. Russell let out a whoop.

"But we didn't find Crusher," said the Kitty Kid sadly.

"No, but *they* did!" Russell said, pointing to the door. Gramps came wheeling into the room. Mr. Curry's grandson, David, was walking beside him, holding a can of soda. Curled up on Gramps's lap was the little calico kitten.

"Crusher!" the Kitty Kid cried as he ran up to Gramps and grabbed his kitten. "Where were you?"

"He walked into the dining room and then he started to sniff around the soda machine. When I wheeled over to investigate, he reached out his paw and tried to claw some ants," Gramps said.

Mrs. Bellucci and Mrs. Furness smiled, and the old people grinned and clapped their hands. The only one who was not smiling was Miss Ruddles. Stony faced, she turned to Mrs. Furness.

"I pride myself on running a clean and orderly nursing home," she snapped. "We cannot allow children and animals to run wild, disturbing the peace of the residents."

"So, who's disturbed?" Gramps asked. "George, are you disturbed?"

Mr. Sipes shook his head. "Heck, no, I'm

not disturbed. I thought it was kind of fun. I'm always up for catching a mouse or two."

"Millie, how about you? Are you disturbed?" Gramps asked, turning to look at Mrs. Barta.

"Why no, Anthony, I like the animals, especially the kitten. It reminds me of the time I had—"

"Yes, Mrs. Barta, I'm sure we've all enjoyed the pets," Miss Ruddles interrupted. "But we do have certain health laws and regulations. We cannot allow insects to overrun the dining room. I am suspending all Pet Days until further notice, and I think it best if the animals leave the building at once."

"How can three ants overrun a dining room?" Gramps muttered. "I'll tell you who's disturbed."

"Shh," Marty's mother whispered, placing her hand on his shoulder.

"Oh, come on, Miss Ruddles," Mr. Grossman spoke up. "At least with the animals we had a little life in the place."

"Unfortunately, Myron, there are some of us who aren't interested in the living, except maybe in a culinary sense," Gramps said, dropping his voice. He shot Marty and Russell a knowing look. "Guard your necks, guard your necks," he whispered.

Marty and Russell began to giggle as they stole a look at Miss Ruddles.

"I think some of us are in need of a nap," she said curtly. "Mrs. Furness, I'll leave it to you to see that the animals are put out of the building." Then she turned and hurried out of the room.

Marty's mother decided that Marty and Russell should wait in the car with Measle and Charlie, while she helped Gramps back to his room.

"But I didn't get to finish my visit with Gramps," Marty complained. He wanted to stay, now that he had found the secret door.

"We'll be back in two weeks, and you can visit then, without my having to worry about missing mice," Mrs. Bellucci told him. "Give Gramps a kiss good-bye now." Marty went up to his grandfather and kissed his cheek.

"I found a secret door," he whispered in his ear. "I think it's the door to Henry Cooper's mailroom."

Gramps nodded and winked. "Next time we'll go on a little tour," he said.

"What was that? What did you say?" Marty's mother asked, leaning over his wheelchair.

"Just about ready for a little snore." Gramps smiled as he patted the white envelope that was sticking out of his pocket. Then he closed his eyes and began to snore loudly, though not nearly as loudly as Mr. Sipes.

Mrs. Bellucci rolled her eyes and pushed the wheelchair down the hall. Gramps turned around for one last wave good-bye. "And remember, guard your necks." They could hear his gravelly whisper between snores.

Martin "Mars Bars" Bellucci and his sidekick Russell the Muscle walked out to the Shady Maples parking lot holding their necks and snoring as loudly as they could.

Chapter 17

Three days later, Marty got off the school bus alone. Russell had stayed home that day complaining of a stomachache. He had eaten an entire jar of pickles the night before on a dare from Devin. Russell was expected to survive, though he doubted that he'd ever be able to look at another pickle.

Marty walked up the steps to his front porch and checked the mailbox. Inside he found four letters. Three of the letters were for his mother. One was from the phone company, another from the electric company, and another from a magazine in New York. One of the letters was for Marty. It was from Abraham Lincoln.

There was no return address on the envelope, but Marty could read the postmark. It said Washington, D.C. He unlocked the front door and ran into the kitchen, throwing the three letters addressed to his mother on the table. Then he slipped off his backpack and raced up to his room. He tore open the envelope and began to read:

Dear Martin "Mars Bars" Bellucci,

Please forgive the brevity of this reply, but as you know I must devote all my energies to the reunification of our great nation. These are troubled times indeed, though I would not make light of the difficulties you are experiencing with your classmates in school.

What I have learned in times of trial is that you are only as strong as you believe yourself to be. With confidence, not muscle, you can lift mountains, but without it you are as powerless as a block of buckeyed wood.

You and your friend Russell are fortunate to have a good horse upon which to ride to school. For all my walking in Illinois as a boy, I'm afraid I've become quite lazy now. Mrs. Lincoln is often urging me to leave my desk and "walk a spell." I'm convinced it's because she fears not that I will grow fat, but that I will forget how to put one foot properly in front of the other. What she fails to understand is that no amount of practice can alter the gait of these naturally clumsy limbs.

I hope you and your grandfather are reunited soon.

Yours,
A. Lincoln

Marty finished reading the letter and took a deep breath. "Abraham Lincoln," he whispered. "I got a letter from"—his voice had risen to a shout—"Abraham Lincoln!"

Measle, who was asleep in his cage, opened one eye as Marty waltzed around the bed with the letter clutched to his chest. Then Marty rushed over to his desk and picked up a pencil and paper. He began to write:

Dear Flame,
  IT CAME!
Danny Reece will go INSANE!

Abraham Lincoln even mentions you. He thinks you have a horse!!! I just got the letter, so if you're feeling okay, come over right away and we can make plans for the showdown with Danny tomorrow.

Your friend,
The Avenger

P.S. Dev told me about the pickles. Cool. Maybe if you could eat just a couple more jars you could get in The G. B. of World Records. We've got a whole new jar of those little round ones, if you want to start practicing right away.

Marty opened his window and sent the message across the line, but Russell's window was closed and his shade was down.

Russ must be down in the den watching TV, Marty decided as he ran downstairs. He picked up the phone in the kitchen and promptly dialed the McGraths' number. After two rings a high-pitched, though deadly serious voice came on the line.

"The McGrath residence; with whom do you wish to speak?"

Marty groaned. It was Deena, Russell's sister, pretending that she was a grown-up again. Deena was only two years older than Marty and Russell, though she considered herself "a much more mature and sophisticated person."

"Deena, it's Marty. Is Russ there?" Marty could hear a little disdainful snort on the other end, followed by, "Hey, pickle breath, it's for you."

Deena still had a ways to go in the sophistication department, Marty thought.

When Russ picked up the phone, Marty told him to run up to his bedroom window and retrieve the secret message. Two minutes later, Russ was racing across the lawn to the Belluccis' yard. Marty rushed out to meet him.

"Oh, wow!" Russ gasped as the two sat on Marty's front porch poring over the letter. "Abraham Lincoln wrote my name. He wrote my name! Look, there it is!"

"I know! I know!" Marty said. "And just think of Danny's face when we show it to him on the bus tomorrow. He'll probably be so shocked that he won't be able to talk."

"Yeah, he'll probably just burst into tears and then hand me his cards." Russell grinned. "His six best cards."

But the next day on the school bus, when Danny Reece read Abraham Lincoln's letter, he only smirked.

"Who are you trying to kid?" He shoved the letter back in Russell's hand. "That's no letter from Abraham Lincoln. You two probably wrote it yourselves last night."

"We did not," Marty objected. "Besides, I have the envelope that it came in. Look, it says Washington, D.C., right on the postmark."

"But there's no return address on it,"

Danny's friend Kyle pointed out. "It doesn't say Abraham Lincoln or even the White House. Your mom probably got a letter from somebody in Washington, and you saved the envelope, and then stuck that phony letter in it."

"That's not true!" Marty shouted. He could feel his face flushing.

"Oh, a letter from Abraham Lincoln is the truth?" Kyle snickered. "Looks like you lost your bet and your famous Six, Russ."

Russell bit down on his lip, trying not to cry.

"Wait a minute," Marty said. "This isn't fair. We've got the letter—"

"You've got *a* letter," Danny interrupted. "But you can't prove it's from Abraham Lincoln or Santa Claus or whoever else you want us to believe it's from."

"But how are we supposed to prove it?" Russ asked. Danny sat staring at his book bag, deep in thought. Finally he looked up and smiled.

"All right, you two Mickey Mouses, here's your last chance," he said. Marty could feel the sweat in his palms as he gripped the bus seat. Russell held his breath.

"You said you could get a letter from anybody, so get another letter, but this time it has to be sent to the school, and it has to be from the Wizard of Menlo Park."

"Thomas Edison?" Russell asked.

"Yeah, Thomas Edison. Of course, he's dead too. But you don't have a problem with that, do you?" Danny sneered. Kyle and Marc Burke, who were sitting with Danny, began to laugh.

"No, no, we don't have a problem with that, do we, Marty?" Russell tried to sound as confident as he could, though Marty could hear the nervousness in his voice. The thought of losing the Six had shaken him badly.

"No problem," Marty said, sinking back in the bus seat.

The Wizard of Menlo Park, he thought. What in the world could he write to the Wizard of Menlo Park?

Chapter 18

Later that day, the two friends were sitting in the reading room, working on their two hundred sentences for Mr. Bullner. They had been working on the same sentences for over a month. Because they fooled around a lot, the sentences were taking them a long time. The boredom of having to write the same words over and over soon began to wear on Marty. He looked up from his paper and yawned.

"You know what we really should be writing?" he said.

"What?" Russ asked.

"The letter to Thomas Edison," Marty said, taking out a clean piece of paper from his notebook. "We'd better get started on it now. My mom is making Gramps a batch of his favorite cookies tonight, and she'll be mailing them tomorrow. I can put the letter in with her package."

"But what if she sees it?" Russ asked.

"I'll seal it in an envelope to Gramps," Marty told him.

"That's a good idea." Russ nodded. "And be sure to put in a note telling your gramps how urgent it is that Henry Cooper deliver the letter. If I lost the Six to Danny Reece, I think I'd die."

"You're not going to die, because Danny is not going to get your Six, don't worry," Marty assured him. "My gramps won't let us down. If he knows the Six are on the line, he'll get the letter mailed."

"You're lucky you've got such a great gramps."

Marty smiled. "I know. There's nobody like my gramps. Now let's see, what should we write?"

"How about, 'Dear Mr. Edison,'" Russell suggested.

"No kidding, Russ." Marty groaned. "I mean after that."

"I sure am glad that you invented the light bulb," Russell continued.

"Um, that's good," Marty said as he began to write.

"Because without light bulbs we wouldn't be able to—oh no . . ." Russell's voice suddenly trailed off. Marty looked up from the letter. He followed Russell's gaze to the reading room door. Mr. Bullner was turning the knob. Both boys knew that he had come to check on their sentences.

It was too late for Marty to make a move. If he tried to hide the letter, Mr. Bullner would demand to see it. And if he saw it, Mr. Bullner would assign them another one hundred sentences. Marty could easily imagine Mr. Bullner making them write: "I will not write to a dead man while I'm supposed to be working on my two hundred sentences."

Marty had to act fast. Mr. Bullner walked into the room, followed by Cara Crimshaw and Allison Meeks, who were there to pick up the overhead projector for Mrs. Riley's third-grade class. Marty slumped over his desk, groaning loudly and clutching his chest.

"What's wrong with Bellucci?" Mr. Bullner demanded as he shot Russell a look. Russell just shook his head. He was as surprised at Marty's outburst as the others were. Meanwhile, Marty continued to groan loudly.

"What's wrong, son?" Mr. Bullner leaned over Marty.

"I think . . . oh, oh, I think I'd better go to the nurse," Marty gasped, being careful to keep his paper covered with his hands. "You know, it feels like a . . . a . . . a cardiac arrest," he whispered, still clutching his chest.

Mr. Bullner looked suspicious. "Cardiac arrest?" he bellowed. "What are you talking about, Bellucci? Ten-year-olds don't get cardiac arrest."

"They don't?" Marty asked in a little voice.

"Of course they don't. You've probably just got a little gas. You'd better go down to the nurse and get checked out. And since the period is almost over, pack up your things and take them with you. McGrath, you can carry them for him." Mr. Bullner walked out of the reading room and headed for the gym. Marty breathed a sigh of relief as he stuffed the papers on his desk back into his notebook.

"You're amazing," Russell whispered. "That was a stroke of genius."

As the two boys headed for the door, a wave of titters and giggles came from behind the overhead projector.

"Hey, Marty, it sounds serious. You don't mind if I tell the rest of the kids in school about your condition, do you?" Allison snickered. Marty gritted his teeth.

"It's just my luck that Allison Meeks has the biggest mouth in the entire school," Marty said as he and Russell walked out of the reading room.

"You've got the best ideas." Russ sighed. "And the worst luck."

That's just what Marty was thinking as he sat down later that night to write his letter to the Wizard of Menlo Park.

Martin Bellucci
% Midbury Elementary School
Midbury, New Hampshire 03301

Dear Thomas Edison,

I sure am glad that you invented the light bulb, because without light bulbs, we'd all have to use candles, and candles are fun but they aren't as bright as a light bulb.

I know you are very busy inventing things, but I was hoping that you could write me back. If you don't, my friend Russell will lose a bet, and he says he'll die if he loses. Russell and I are ten years old, and I was hoping to grow up with him. So please write.

I think your light bulb was a good idea. I have good ideas all the time, but somehow things always seem to go wrong. Did you ever have this problem?

When things used to go wrong, I could always talk to my gramps about it. But he's sick now and lives far away. I had fun visiting him the last time, but it's not the same as having him around. My mom says she misses his pancakes. Gramps used to make the best pan-

cakes. I think you would like my gramps. He is a great talker, and he's good at changing light bulbs too.

Your friend,
Martin Bellucci (My gramps calls me Mars Bars.)

P.S. Someday I hope to have as great an idea as your light bulb, without anything going wrong.

Chapter 19

"Do you think it's all right?" Marty asked after reading the letter aloud. But there was no reply. "Russ? Will you come out from under there and tell me what you think of the letter?" Marty called.

Russell was under Marty's bed. The two were having a sleepover. Whenever he spent the night at Marty's, Russ crawled under Marty's bed to see what kind of good stuff was lying around.

"Russ, did you hear me?" Marty said. "What do you think of the letter?"

"It's good, it's good," came a muffled voice. "I like the part where you mention me. Hey, here's that red marble you lost after Christmas, and did you know that you've got half a bag of chocolate chip cookies under here? How old do you think they are?"

"The marble is probably newer than the cookies," Marty said as he put the letter into an envelope along with a note to Gramps. He could hear his mother's footsteps in the hall. "Finished in the nick of time," Marty whispered, sealing the envelope. The bedroom door opened, and Mrs. Bellucci looked in.

"It's time for bed, boys," she called, surveying the room. "Marty, where's Russell? I thought he was going to spend the night."

"He's spending it looking for old cookies," Marty told her, pointing to the two small feet that were sticking out from under the bed.

"Russell, come out from there!" Mrs. Bellucci exclaimed. "Don't you dare go eating any old cookies. Haven't you put your poor stomach through enough with all those pickles?"

"Hey, Russ, maybe we could get you in *The Guinness Book of World Records* for eating the oldest cookies." Marty laughed.

"Even I don't want to get in the book that bad," Russ said, getting to his feet and handing Mrs. Bellucci the crumpled bag. She plucked a dust ball from his hair and shook her head.

"It's time to get *in* bed now, not under it," she ordered, pointing to the made-up cot beside Marty's bed. Russell did as he was told and dove under the cot's cozy blankets.

Marty handed his mother the envelope. "Mom, could you send this with your package to Gramps?"

"Sure," she replied. "Gramps loves getting your letters." Marty and Russell grinned. Mrs. Bellucci was about to turn off the light when she spotted the bluebird house sitting on Marty's bookshelf.

"Oh." She sighed wistfully. "You never did get to hang your birdhouse, did you?" Marty didn't answer. "If you'd like to, we can get the ladder out this weekend and hang it up then," she offered.

Marty frowned. "No, I don't think so. I'm going to wait for Gramps." Mrs. Bellucci started to say something, but then she looked over at Russell and changed her mind.

"We'll talk about it later," she said, turning off the light. Marty and Russell listened to her footsteps on the stairs. They waited until they heard the sound of the television set going on in the living room. Then Marty leaned over and pulled out his flashlight from behind his bed while Russell tiptoed across the room.

They shone the light into Measle's cage. The two special agents were curled up in a corner, fast asleep.

"I wonder how they get so tired out?" Russell whispered. "It's not like they had to take gym today or anything."

"I don't know about Charlie, but Measle is always exercising," Marty said.

"The only thing that Charlie exercises are his teeth," Russell complained.

"So why don't you want your mom to help you hang the birdhouse?" he asked.

Marty tiptoed over to the bookshelf and picked up the little wooden house. He carefully carried it back to his bed. "Remember when my gramps helped me make it?" Marty whispered. Russ nodded. "Well, we planned this whole special kind of celebration. I have to wait for Gramps. When he gets better, he'll help me hang it, and then we'll have blueberry pancakes in bed while we watch the bluebirds. It's going to be really neat."

"That does sound neat, but what if he doesn't get better?" Russell asked. "Deena says that people who go into nursing homes never come out."

Marty felt his throat tightening. "That's a lie," he said hotly. "Deena doesn't know everything. My gramps is just staying there until he's better."

"Okay, okay, you don't have to get so worked up about it," Russell said. "Why don't we fool around with the birdhouse?" he suggested, trying to change the subject. "Maybe we could put Measle and Charlie in it."

"No, it's already full," Marty told him as he lifted the birdhouse door and reached inside. He began pulling things out and placing them on the bed. "Until it gets hung up, it makes a good place to hide all my special stuff. See, I've got my two best marbles, the Indian arrowhead that I found last summer, my best woodpecker feather, and the letters." He carefully placed the letters from Napoleon and Abraham Lincoln on his pillow.

"I hope you have another letter to put in there soon." Russ sighed. "I'll die if I lose the Six, I really will."

"I wish you'd quit saying that," Marty told him. "You don't have to die. I told you the letter will come."

But later that night as he snuggled down under his blankets, Marty wasn't so sure. He suddenly wasn't sure about a lot of things. What if the Wizard of Menlo Park didn't write back? What if Russ lost his Six to Danny Reece? And what if Deena was right? What if Gramps was never coming home?

Marty closed his eyes tight and watched the little beams of light breaking over the blackness. It was then that he remembered his letter to Vincent van Gogh. It was still in his desk at school. He opened his eyes and leaned his head back, looking up at *Starry Night* above his bed. He had to squint in the darkness in order to see it. He didn't know why, but the little starry explosions of light that filled the dark canvas made him feel better.

Chapter 20

"Oh, please let this be it," Russell whispered a little more than a week later as he and Marty sat in their classroom, watching the secretary walk through the door. Both boys leaned forward in their seats. The secretary handed Miss Gerbino an envelope. As she read the return address, Miss Gerbino's mouth formed a surprised O.

"Marty, could you please come up to my desk?" she called.

"Yes! Yes! Yes!" Russell whispered excitedly, turning around in his seat to grin at Danny Reece.

"Marty, did you write another letter?" Miss Gerbino asked. Marty nodded.

"And to whom did you write this letter?" Miss Gerbino asked.

Marty coughed and then fidgeted in place. "To—to the Wizard of Menlo Park," he muttered.

"The Wizard of Menlo Park? Thomas Alva Edison, that Wizard of Menlo Park?" Miss Gerbino's voice was getting higher and higher.

"Not another dead guy." The secretary groaned.

"Yes, that's the one," Marty said, trying to smile. But Miss Gerbino had a dazed look on her face as she read the return address aloud.

"Thomas A. Edison, West Orange, New Jersey. And the postmark says West Orange, New Jersey, too!" Everyone in the classroom whispered excitedly as Miss Gerbino handed Marty the letter. He quickly opened it, and everyone was silent as he began to read it out loud.

EDISON LABORATORY

Dear Martin,

I received your urgent letter. I hope this arrives in time, so that your friend Russell does not have to depart this life.

I fully sympathize with your plight of having so many good ideas go wrong. It has been just so with all of my inventions. I can't tell you the number of times that things have taken a wrong turn and seemed most hopeless, only to eventually right themselves after much hard work. A great inventor needs not only great ideas, but a full dose of patience and determination.

When I was about your age and living in Port Huron, I attended a two-story schoolhouse. Well, it wasn't long before a great idea came to me. I decided to sneak a baited fishing hook into school along with some string. While the schoolmaster's back was turned, a friend and I lowered the hook out an open window to see what we could catch. And within minutes, we felt a tugging on the line. We quickly pulled it up, and much to our surprise, found that we had caught a chicken! Well, its wings were flapping and its feathers were flying, and before long, the whole school was in an uproar. That "good idea" earned me the switch from both the schoolmaster and my mother. Great ideas take much hard work. You have to think things through, and even then you may end up pulling in a chicken or two every now and then!

My regards to your grandfather.

Thomas Edison

P.S. When I was a boy my mother called me Alva, my friends called me Al, and my sister called me Rinkey.

Marty's heart raced as he looked up from the letter. His teacher and classmates were staring at him in awe. Even the secretary's mouth had dropped open. There was an eerie stillness in the classroom as everyone stopped breathing. The silence was suddenly broken by Danny Reece's anxious voice.

"That can't be real!" he cried. "That can't be

a letter from Thomas Edison, can it, Miss Gerbino?" Miss Gerbino blinked, not knowing what to say. Finally she was able to sputter, "Marty, I think I'll need to speak with your mother tonight."

Oh, great, Marty thought. Russ gets to win his bet, and I get in trouble with my mom.

Later that night, Marty's mother called Marty into the kitchen. She had just hung up from talking to Miss Gerbino.

"Martin Bellucci, what is all this about letters from dead people?" she demanded. Marty sat down at the kitchen table. He started licking the icing off the chocolate cake in front of him.

"Marty, I'm waiting," said his mother. "And please stop eating all the frosting."

Marty took a long time to swallow, then said, "I didn't do anything wrong. I just wrote some letters to some famous people."

"Famous *dead* people?" Mrs. Bellucci asked.

"Yeah, I guess they were kind of dead," Marty muttered.

"Kind of dead? Napoleon isn't *kind of* dead, Marty. Thomas Edison isn't *kind of* dead! Those men *are* dead!" Mrs. Bellucci cried.

"Well, yeah, I guess so," Marty said.

"Then you can't possibly be getting letters back from them, not if they're dead."

"But they did write back! I can show you the letters," Marty protested.

"No, Marty. Someone else had to have written you those letters. Miss Gerbino said that it couldn't have been you or one of the kids in your class because the writing was too grown up. And then there're the postmarks. Someone actually mailed you a letter from France?"

"That was Napoleon," Marty told her.

"No, no, Marty." His mother sighed. "We just went over that. Napoleon is dead, and when people die, they can't write to you."

"But Mom, just let me show you the letters. Once you see them, you'll believe me." Marty raced up to his room, and within minutes he was back in the kitchen, handing her the three envelopes.

Mrs. Bellucci sat down at the kitchen table

and began to read. She brought her hand up to her forehead, sighing several times.

"This just doesn't make any sense. It makes no sense at all." She looked up at Marty. "Where did you mail the letters from? Did you put them in our mailbox?"

"No," Marty mumbled.

"Then you must have sent them from the post office. But how did you get to the post office?" Marty squirmed in his seat. "Marty, did someone help you mail those letters?"

Marty took a deep breath before answering. "Yes," he replied.

"Now, this is very important. This is no time to be making up stories. I want the truth, Marty. Who helped you mail the letters?"

Marty felt the tears coming to his eyes. He didn't know how he was going to tell the truth and still keep his promise to Gramps. He looked up at his mother and bit down on his lip. Maybe he could tell her just part of it.

"Gramps," he whispered. "Gramps helped me mail the letters."

"Oh, I should have known!" Mrs. Bellucci exclaimed. "I should have guessed that he was the one who cooked up something this crazy."

"But he didn't cook it up. Honest, Mom!" Marty cried. "Henry Cooper had the secret mailroom and Gramps just found out about it."

"Henry Cooper? Who's Henry Cooper? And what's this about a secret mailroom?"

Marty leaned back in his chair. He hadn't meant to, but he had broken his promise. With a sigh, he told his mother the rest of what had happened: how Gramps had given the letters to Henry Cooper and how Cooper's Secret Courier Service had gone through time to deliver them.

"Oh no," Mrs. Bellucci exclaimed when Marty had finished. "This time, he's really gone too far." She reached across the table and grabbed Marty's hands. "I know how much you love your gramps," she told him. "And I know how much you love his stories, but you're getting too old for this kind of thing. It's not the truth, Marty. It's just a story."

"But if it's just a story, who wrote the letters?" Marty said. "Look how different the handwriting is in each one."

"You're right, it is different," Mrs. Bellucci

agreed, looking over the letters. "Maybe Gramps got some of the other residents to write them for him," she suggested. "You know how friendly he is with everyone at the home."

Marty frowned. "But then how do you explain the postmark from Paris, France? And Washington, D.C.?" he asked, his face brightening. Mrs. Bellucci squinted as she sat thinking.

"I don't know, I just don't . . ." Suddenly she smiled. "Marty, do you remember Pet Day? Do you remember Mrs. Barta, the old woman who had been a puppeteer?" Marty nodded. "Well, where did she say she was from? And where did she tell us her family was still living?" Marty tried to remember.

"France," he whispered. "She said she had family living in Paris, France."

Chapter 21

"And Miss Hillvaney has relatives living in New Jersey! Wasn't that where her great-niece was from?" Mrs. Bellucci asked. Marty reluctantly nodded.

"That only leaves the letter from Washington, D.C. Now let me think. Who had relatives in Washington?" Marty's mother mused.

"Mr. Sipes," Marty said. "Mr. Sipes got rid of the cockroaches in the White House."

"Yes, that's right." Mrs. Bellucci's head bobbed up and down. "Mrs. Furness did say that his son had taken over the business. Oh, Marty, don't you see? Gramps must have asked his friends in the home to get their relatives to mail you answers to your letters from the right places. It's so like him to do something crazy like that."

"But why?" Marty's voice was beginning to crack as the tears rolled down his cheeks. "Why did he have to do it? Why did he have to lie?"

His mother reached out and wiped a tear from his face. "You know what a storyteller your gramps is, hon. To him, it's not lying. To him, it's like telling you about Santa Claus."

"But I'm too big to believe in Santa Claus," Marty protested.

"I know you are, but I guess it's Gramps's way of keeping you small for a little longer. He loves you so much that I guess he wants you to have the most magical childhood you can. That's why he's always telling you stories and cooking up all kinds of plans—not to lie to you, but to show you how special life is. I'm not saying what he did was right. I'm just trying to explain that what he did was out of love. I know he would never do anything to hurt you."

Marty picked up a paper napkin from the table and blew his nose. "I guess a part of me never believed that it could really be true," he said between sniffles. "He sure went through a lot of trouble to get all those letters just right, though."

"Yes, your grandfather is pretty amazing. But I'm going to tell him that he's got to stop. Telling the truth is very important, Marty. It's all right to tell stories as long as people know they're stories. Besides, Gramps has to face the fact that you're growing up."

"No!" Marty cried. "You can't. I mean, I promised him I wouldn't tell. Besides, what harm could it do not to tell him? All this time, he's wanted to let me pretend, so why can't I let him pretend now?"

"Do you mean that you want to pretend that the letters are real?"

"Yes, just for Gramps," Marty replied. "I think it would make him happy."

Marty's mother smiled. "It's funny, but I think you're right. Somehow, when he gets all wrapped up in one of his stories, it's almost like a part of him gets to believe, too. To be a kid again."

"And he loves to see the letters," Marty

said. "I can bring him the latest one when we go to Shady Maples tomorrow. I've even got another letter already written. This one is to Vincent van Gogh."

"A letter to Vincent van Gogh! How did I end up with such a crazy family!" Mrs. Bellucci exclaimed. "Well, I guess you can bring it, as long as you understand that Vincent van Gogh won't really be writing back. And that letter will probably be written by Miss Hillvaney, or Mr. Sipes, or any one of Gramps's friends."

"I know, I know," Marty assured her.

"Oh, and one more thing," Mrs. Bellucci said. "You're going to have to tell the kids in your class the truth. That includes Danny Reece. Miss Gerbino told me about the bet with Russell."

Marty frowned. "Does that mean Russ will have to give Danny his Special Six?" he asked anxiously.

"No, I don't think so. If you'd like me to, I can call Danny's parents and explain what happened. But this should be a lesson to you both about making bets."

"Oh, don't worry, Mom, we learned our lesson," Marty assured her.

That night an urgent message was sent from the Avenger to the Flame.

Dear Flame,

I just found out that the letters from the dead guys weren't real. My mom figured out who's been sending them. It was my gramps. He had his friends at the home help him. At first I was mad at him for doing it, but then my mom explained why he did it, and I'm not too mad anymore, just disappointed. It's a long story and I'll tell you the rest tomorrow. But my mom says that you don't have to give Danny the Six. She said she would talk to Danny's parents about it for you.

I should have known the letters were fakes, especially after the one from Thomas Edison. Whoever heard of a famous inventor having such a goofy nickname as Rinkey? I guess my gramps just got carried away. I hope you aren't mad or anything. We're going to Shady Maples tomorrow, but I'm not taking Measle. He's probably still having nightmares about

Crusher, so send Special Agent Charlie, if he
wants to sleep over.

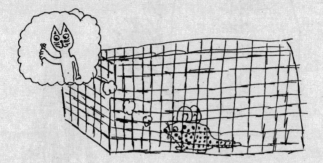

Your friend,
The Avenger

Dear Avenger,
   Boy, are we going to look stupid on the bus
on Monday after all the kids find out about the
letters! I wish your gramps had never done
this. But there's one thing I don't understand.
What about the secret door? You did see it,
didn't you? If it wasn't a door to the mailroom,
what was it? I guess I'm not too mad, but if I
had lost the Six, I don't care what Mr. Bullner
says, I would have had cardiac arrest for sure!

Dear Flame,

I asked my mom about the secret door, and she said that Shady Maples is an old building and they probably did a lot of remodeling, adding on rooms and stuff. Gramps is in the new wing, but she said they have a whole other old wing. The rooms in that part of the home are all empty and they're planning on tearing them down. The door probably leads to the old wing. She said M. R. must have stood for Men's Room.

I'll see you when I get back from visiting Gramps. I hope you aren't mad anymore. I put Charlie in the cage with Measle and he and Measle are having a contest to see who can scratch himself in the weirdest spot.

The Avenger

Chapter 22

On Saturday morning, Marty folded his letters from Thomas Edison and to Vincent van Gogh and shoved them into his pocket. Then he got out his backpack for the trip to Shady Maples. He packed two action figures, his colored markers and a pad of paper, a magnet, a nail, two rubber bands, two cat stickers, and a Band-Aid. It was a long trip to the nursing home, and he wanted to have enough interesting stuff with him so that he wouldn't get bored.

His mother gave him two apples, a bag of oatmeal cookies, and an orange. She had also picked up two books at the library. One was a ghost story, and the other was a book on the life of Thomas Edison. Mrs. Bellucci knew that

Marty was studying the inventor in school, and she thought he might like to read a little more about him.

Once Marty and his mother started on the trip, Marty ate a few of the cookies and one of the apples. Then he took out his action figures and began to play with them. After that, he took out his markers and paper and drew a man with little orange ears and a giant belly button. The belly button took up most of the man's stomach and was green. Marty gave the man purple teeth and a square yellow nose. He started on another drawing, this time of the man's dog, but when he tried to draw the dog's belly button, it didn't look right. Marty sat wondering if dogs even had belly buttons.

Marty put his markers and paper in his pack. He stared at the highway that stretched out before them. It looked as if it could go on forever.

"Are we almost there?" he groaned.

Mrs. Bellucci was singing along to a song on the radio and didn't hear him at first.

"*Stop, in the name of love*, huh?" Mrs. Bellucci turned her head to look at him. "Did you say something?"

"I said, are we almost there?" Marty repeated.

"Oh no, we've only gone about halfway. Why don't you read one of the books I got you from the library?" she suggested. "It will help to pass the time."

Marty glanced down at the two books on the seat and frowned, then stared back out at the highway. He was hoping to see a red pickup truck, but the only trucks he saw were tractor-trailers. He turned around and looked at the empty backseat.

Gramps could have the whole backseat to himself for the ride home, Marty thought. He could even lie down if he was tired, and he could use my jacket for a pillow. Marty closed his eyes and wished with all his heart. Let him come home with us today. Let him come home.

"Here, why don't you try this one?" Mrs. Bellucci said, as she handed one of the books to him. Marty looked at the cover. In bold red letters it said, THE BIOGRAPHY OF THOMAS

EDISON. Marty pulled another oatmeal cookie out of the bag and opened the book. Biting into the cookie, he began to read.

Thomas Alva Edison was born on February 11, 1847, in the small town of Milan, Ohio. While his mother called him Alva, his friends called him Al, and his sister called him Rinkey.

Marty almost choked on his cookie when he read the name "Rinkey." Little bits of oatmeal cookie crumbs went flying into the air as he began to cough.

"Are you all right?" his mother asked.

"His nickname really was Rinkey!" Marty gasped, pointing down to the book.

"Who? What are you talking about?"

Marty went on to explain his Edison letter and how he thought Gramps had made up the nickname. "But it says it right here, in this book!" Marty exclaimed. "His nickname really was Rinkey!"

"It does sort of sound like a name Gramps would make up," Mrs. Bellucci had to admit.

"I guess he knows a lot more about Thomas Edison than we suspected. It's amazing, the enormous collection of facts that your grandfather has stored in his head over the years."

Maybe, Marty was thinking. Or maybe some other strange thing was going on. He knew his mother was probably right, but he suddenly found himself wondering again. What if Gramps hadn't known? After all, Gramps had never told him about Thomas Edison. He had told him stories about so many different people, surely he would have mentioned Edison. What if Gramps really didn't know? Marty spent the rest of the trip reading about Thomas Edison and wondering about his letter.

As Mrs. Bellucci turned the car into the Shady Maples parking lot, Marty could see a number of residents sitting in their wheelchairs on the big front porch. His mother climbed the brick steps to the door while Marty trotted beside her on the wide concrete ramp that ended by the top step.

He looked for Gramps on the porch but he wasn't there. Marty was glad to see Mr. Curry, though (glad to see that he hadn't died). The old man was smiling. His head was thrown back and his face was warmed by the sun. Beside him, in another wheelchair, sat Mr. Sipes. His head hung over his chest, and he was snoring so loudly, most of the other residents had moved away.

"Hello, Mr. Curry, how are you feeling?" Mrs. Bellucci called as she and Marty stood by the door. Mr. Curry waved and shook his head. Then he reached up to his ear and adjusted his hearing aid.

"I turn it off when Sipes is around," he explained, with a nod to Mr. Sipes. "With him snoring away to beat the band, I'm likely to lose the little hearing I have left. It's hard on the eardrums, you know." Marty and his mother both laughed as they watched him turn off his hearing aid with a shrug. Marty followed his mother through the door and down the long hallway to Gramps's room. They stopped to say hello to Miss Hillvaney, who was sitting in her wheelchair in front of the recreation room.

"Shhh," she whispered, "the babies are nap-

ping. They were up all night. It's the croup."
Marty and his mother nodded, as if they understood.

I don't think she could have written one of the letters, Marty thought as they continued down the hall. When they finally reached Gramps's room, Marty knew something was wrong, since the room was dark. The curtains were drawn and the lights were off. Gramps was lying in bed with his eyes closed. He was breathing in short, irregular gasps. To Marty it sounded as if his grandfather were underwater.

And Gramps doesn't look so good, Marty thought as he stepped up to the foot of the bed. Gramps's skin had a yellow tint to it and his eyelids were red and puffy. Marty could see the worried look on his mother's face, and he knew that this was one more day that Gramps wouldn't be coming home. Once more his wish wasn't going to come true.

A nurse came into the room and in hushed whispers she explained to Mrs. Bellucci that Gramps had had "a bad night" and that his pain medication had been increased. "He'll probably sleep most of the day," the nurse said.

"We've come so far, and we won't be able to come again until next week," Marty's mother whispered. "I'd just like to sit with him for a while, if that's all right." The nurse nodded and said that the doctor had been in to see Gramps and was at the nurses' station now, if Marty's mother wanted to talk to him. After the nurse left the room, Mrs. Bellucci motioned for Marty to come and stand beside her at the side of the bed.

"It's good that Gramps is finally able to rest," his mother said. But Marty could tell from the tone of her voice that she was worried. "Even though his eyes are closed, he may know that we're here," she whispered, placing her hand on Gramps's arm. "And he'll rest easier if he knows that we're close."

Marty gently laid his small hand over Gramps's outstretched fingers. Marty and his mother stood there for a long while, not saying anything.

"Why don't you sit in that chair by the window?" said Mrs. Bellucci. "I'm going to go speak to the doctor."

Marty sat down on the big leather chair. He shoved his hands into his back pocket, feeling for his folded letters. Then he looked at the bed.

Come on, Gramps, stop breathing so funny, and wake up, Marty thought. Then he had another thought. What if Gramps could hear him? What if the medication made him so drowsy that he couldn't open his eyes, but his ears still worked? Marty pulled one of the letters out of his pocket and stood up. He walked over to the bed.

"Gramps, can you hear me?" he whispered, tugging on Gramps's pajama sleeve. But his grandfather's only reply was a series of short gasps, followed by a gargly sound in his throat.

"If you can hear me, Gramps," Marty continued, "I just want you to know that I got a letter from Thomas Edison, and it was really neat. Would you like me to read it to you?" There was no answer, but Marty unfolded the letter anyway, and laid it on the bed. Then he slipped one of his hands underneath Gramps's hand and slowly began to read aloud. He stopped at the funny parts, where he knew Gramps would stop to laugh, the part about the chicken and the fishing line, and the part about the great inventor's nickname.

"Rinkey, isn't that a goofy nickname?" Marty giggled, looking down at the letter. He was imagining Gramps's smile, and the way his eyes lit up behind his big, thick reading glasses. But when Marty raised his head, he found his grandfather's expression unchanged. Gramps wasn't smiling, and his eyes were shut tight. Marty folded the letter and placed it back in his pocket.

"And I've got one more letter for Henry Cooper to deliver, Gramps," Marty whispered. "This one is to Vincent van Gogh." He opened the letter and put it on the bed. Just then, Mrs. Bellucci walked into the room. Her forehead was full of wrinkles and her eyes were brimming with tears.

"Marty, if you don't mind, I think we should spend the day with Gramps," she said.

"Is he going to wake up soon?" Marty asked hopefully.

"No, hon, I don't think so. The doctor said that Gramps is very, very sick," his mother whispered. There was so much sadness in her voice, Marty wanted to ask if Gramps would ever wake up, but he couldn't bring himself to say the words. He looked down at the letter on the bed and listened to Gramps's short, raspy breaths.

What could he do with the letter, if he couldn't give it to Gramps? he wondered. What good was a letter to Vincent van Gogh? Marty noticed the wastepaper basket next to the bed. Tears filled his eyes as he thought about crumpling up the letter and throwing it away. Suddenly he felt Gramps's fingers tighten around his hand. It lasted only a moment, but Marty knew that Gramps was trying to tell him something.

"Why don't you go on down to the dining room and get a soda?" Mrs. Bellucci suggested, reaching into her purse and pulling out some coins.

Marty slipped his hand out from under Gramps's big fingers, folded his letter, and stuffed it back into his pocket. He took the money his mother gave him and walked out into the hall. At any other time, having a soda would have made him smile. But now it didn't really appeal to him all that much.

When Marty reached the big machine in the dining room, he mechanically deposited the coins and pushed the first button that his fingers touched. He saw the bright green-and-gold can drop down and realized that he had gotten a diet soda. Marty hated diet sodas. He picked up the cold can and shrugged. He would give it to his mother.

I'm not really thirsty anyway, Marty thought as he left the dining room. As he started back to Gramps's room, he passed an open door on his left. He peeked inside. It was a closet. Marty realized that it was the same closet where he had searched for Measle and Charlie, the closet with the secret door.

Marty suddenly had an idea. He quickly surveyed the empty hallway, then quietly disappeared into the closet, turning on the light and closing the door behind him.

Chapter 23

I know Mom is right, Marty told himself as he climbed the stepladder that stood in front of the shelves of towels and sheets. This door probably leads to the other wing of the nursing home. He began to push stacks of freshly laundered linen aside until he could see the cracked gold letters M. R. Marty felt a chill run down his back. He pressed his ear to the door and listened. Was that a faint buzzing sound coming from the other side? Or was he imagining it? Marty listened again, but heard nothing this time.

I guess Mom was right about the M. R. standing for Men's Room, thought Marty, staring at the letters. But mothers can't always be right, can they? What if, just this once, she were wrong?

Marty jumped down from the stepladder and looked under the bottom shelf. He could see the crack between the old door and the floor. Marty pulled the folded letter out of his back pocket.

"Henry Cooper," he whispered, "I know you're probably not real, but just in case you are and you're in there, please see that this gets mailed to Vincent van Gogh." He shoved the letter under the door. Then he put his ear close to the crack and listened. When no sounds came, he got to his feet, grabbed his can of soda, turned off the light, and walked out into the hall, closing the closet door behind him as quietly as he could.

Chapter 24

On Sunday morning Marty opened his eyes and looked at his alarm clock. It said 8:00 A.M. He closed his eyes and listened to the noises coming from the kitchen. He knew that his mother must be making breakfast.

With his eyes shut tight, Marty pretended that his mother was still sleeping in her room and that down in the kitchen, it was Gramps who was making breakfast, just as he had always done before he had gotten sick and moved to Shady Maples.

Marty could hear the sounds of water running and plates clinking. He smiled as he heard the refrigerator door open and shut. A warm, cozy feeling spread over him as he imagined Gramps making a big pitcher of orange juice. Suddenly he could hear the old gravelly comforting voice.

"You've got to have your O.J. in the morning, Mars Bars. Keeps the hair on your chest."

"But Gramps, I don't have any hair on my chest," Marty imagined himself answering.

"No kidding?" Gramps's eyebrows arched dramatically. "Well, I do happen to have some secret hair-inducing blueberries that I can throw into these pancakes. Should fix you right up. These will put the fuzz on for sure."

"Blueberries? Fuzz?" Marty giggled.

Now Marty could smell the aroma of hot, buttery pancakes. Marty took a deep breath. He opened his eyes. He really did smell pancakes! But how could that be? Marty knew that his mother didn't like to cook all that much. The one time she had actually tried to make pancakes, she had burned them so badly, the whole kitchen had filled with smoke. Gramps had called her a fire hazard. After Gramps moved to Shady Maples, they would eat cereal for breakfast.

Marty sat up and took another deep breath. Definitely pancakes, and if his mother wasn't

making them, who was? Marty began to grin.
It must be Gramps! he thought excitedly.
Gramps must be back! The doctor must have
cured him with all that medication, and now
he was well and had come back to them!

Marty's heart pounded as he sprang out of
bed and flew down the stairs. My wish came
true! My wish came true, he thought. He
couldn't wait to see Gramps back in the
kitchen, back where he belonged.

"Gramps, your pancakes smell great. I'm
coming, Gramps, I'm coming!" he called, running down the hallway. But when he reached
the kitchen, it was his mother who was standing at the stove, not Gramps. Marty stood fro-
zen in the doorway, too stunned to talk.

"Oh, Marty, I'm so sorry," his mother said,
seeing the disappointment on his face and re-
alizing what he must have thought when he
smelled the pancakes.

"He's not back, then?" Marty mumbled. His
mother came and put her arm around him.

"No, hon, and he won't be coming back,"
she said softly, her eyes glassy with tears. "I
got a call from Miss Ruddles early this morning. Gramps died in his sleep last night."

Marty's chest heaved painfully. He felt like someone had punched him hard. When he tried to talk, he had to struggle to get the words out before they were broken by the sob that was welling up in his throat.

"Oh no, not Gramps," Marty croaked. "He can't be gone. He wouldn't leave without me."

"He didn't have any choice, hon. It was his time to die," Mrs. Bellucci said gently.

"But I didn't get to tell him about the last letter, the one to Vincent." Marty felt the tears falling down his face. "And I'll never get to tell him anything anymore, will I?"

Through his tears, Marty could see his mother crying as she shook her head no. Suddenly, he couldn't hold back any longer. His mother pulled him toward her and together they stood sobbing in each other's arms. They stood there for a long while, until the smoke from the burning pancakes began to fill the room.

"Oh no, I've done it again!" Mrs. Bellucci exclaimed as she wiped her eyes with her apron and rushed to turn off the grill. "I wanted to make a special breakfast for us today. One that Gramps would have liked to make," she explained as she scraped the burned pancakes off the grill.

"I think the grill was too hot. I've got some more batter; should I try again?" Marty stood thinking this over. He wasn't all that hungry, but the thought of eating pancakes was something comforting. He nodded, and as his mother stirred the batter, he silently opened the freezer and took out a bag of blueberries. He carried them over to the stove.

"For the fuzz," he whispered. As the tears fell down his cheeks, he began dropping blueberries into the batter, one by one.

Chapter 25

In the days and weeks that followed, Marty felt like crying a lot. He decided that sometimes it was okay to cry and sometimes it wasn't. It was okay to cry at the memorial service for Gramps, because there seemed to be a lot of people crying there. And it was okay to cry at home, when the only person who could see him was his mother. But he didn't think it was okay to cry in school or on the bus, even though he felt like crying there too. He didn't want the other kids to see him.

One day on his way to school, Marty was looking out the window as the bus came to a stop on Henly Street. A number of first and second graders were waiting in line. There were mothers and grandmothers standing to the side talking, and an older, bald-headed man had bent down to tie one of the first grader's sneakers.

Marty's heart began to race as he recognized the brown sweater the man was wearing. Even though the man's back was to him, Marty knew immediately whose bald head and big ears those were. He pressed his face to the window and was about to call out, "Gramps!" when the man stood up. He turned around, and Marty could see at once that his nose was a little too straight and his lips were a little too thin. The man looked like Gramps, but he was someone else.

Marty sank back in his seat, shaken. It wasn't Gramps and it would never be Gramps. What was that stranger doing looking so much like him? Why was he alive and Gramps dead? A wave of sadness washed over Marty once again. He wondered if the heavy, sad feeling he had in his chest would ever go away.

Weeks went by, and Marty felt no better. Even Russell noticed.

"Everything is so different now," Russ said one day after they had gotten off the bus. "We don't have fun like we used to."

Marty shrugged. He knew Russ was right. They hadn't been fooling around anymore, and though this kept them out of trouble with Mr. Bullner, things seemed boring and dull. They had even stopped sending secret messages to each other on the line. Marty knew that he wasn't fun to be with, and he didn't like being that way, but he didn't know what to do about it.

"Why don't you come over and play Creeps in the Castle?" Russell suggested. "We haven't played that in a long time."

"Not today; I'm kind of tired," Marty told him. Russell frowned and walked into his house. Marty continued down the sidewalk. When he reached his front porch, he searched for the house key and opened the door. He threw his backpack down on the floor and dropped the key on the hall table.

He turned on the television in the living room and began flicking through the channels. He finally stopped at a game show. It was called "Family Fun." There were two families that competed against each other, trying to answer questions on different topics.

Marty lay down on the couch and stared at the families on the show. One had a mother and a father and three grown children. The other family had a young girl who was about Marty's age. She was standing next to the announcer. Marty noticed that there were no old people. He raised the volume on the set. The families were answering questions about history.

"All right, here's your next question," the announcer barked. "In the year 1814, Napoleon Bonaparte was exiled to an island from which he later escaped. What was the name of that island?"

Marty sprang up from the couch. "Elba!" he shouted. Instead of the girl, Marty suddenly saw himself standing next to the announcer on the TV screen. His mother and Gramps were there, too!

"Yes! Yes! Yes!" the announcer cried. "You've got that right. And now, for your final game point, what is the name of the island on which Napoleon died?" There was a moment of tense silence. Marty was so excited, he couldn't think, but then he saw Gramps leaning toward him.

"St. Helena," Gramps whispered with a wink.

"St. Helena," Marty called out. A loud buzzer sounded, and the audience went wild, since he and Gramps and Mom had just won the game. They were the winning family on "Family Fun!"

But just as Marty had seen himself with his mother and Gramps, they were gone, and he was left staring at the other smiling family. The television family. The family that had really won.

When a commercial came on, Marty blinked and looked around at the empty house, which felt even emptier without Gramps. He decided not to watch "Family Fun" anymore and turned on some cartoons instead.

After the cartoon show was over, Marty turned off the television set and headed up to his room to talk to Measle. On his way, he noticed the house key still sitting on the hall table. Marty's mother was always reminding him to bring the key inside, so he picked it up now and carried it back to the porch.

He placed the key under the flowerpot and remembered that he hadn't checked the mail. He flipped open the mailbox and stuck his hand inside. There was only one letter in the box. Marty pulled it out and glanced at the big black brushstrokes that spelled his name. He blinked several times as he read the postmark. Arles, France.

Who lives in Arles, France? he wondered as he carried the letter up to his room. Marty flopped down on his bed and tore open the envelope. He pulled out a rough sheet of ragged brown paper.

"Dear Martin," he began to read.

I am glad that you like my paintings. So few people do. My brother, Theo, has shown some of these paintings, and it is rare when people express such appreciation. You are right, I do know something of sadness. It sometimes over-

whelms my life, and yet in my painting, I can break through to the joy that is always there waiting.

I will tell you a secret, my friend. When I am happiest is when I'm not wishing for things to be different. Wishing for this or that won't bring much joy, for we often don't get all that we wish for. But accepting all that we do have and seeing the good in it is another thing entirely.

I have so little money that I could not buy proper paper on which to write this letter and had to make do with this brown scrap that was wrapped around a pair of shoes I purchased from a cobbler.

Now instead of wishing for a finer, whiter stationery, I've begun to see just how very beautiful this coarse-grained paper is. Can you see the golden light in the brown? Feel the richness in the texture. See how well the black ink strokes contrast with the nut-brown color of the paper. Aren't we fortunate to have stumbled on so much beauty?

From your letter I can feel your sadness at being separated from your grandfather. I have

spent much time feeling lonely and separated
from others myself. But in my best moments, I
feel the presence of those I've loved, and then
I feel less lonely. They live in my heart, for you
see, I believe that we cannot live on this earth
without leaving it changed in some way. If you
need to be with your grandfather, don't wish
for what you can't have. Enjoy what you do
have, the presence of his spirit. When someone
touches your heart very deeply, they can never
really leave you. They're part of you and how
you see the world.

> Your friend,
> Vincent

P.S. When I'm out walking on moonless nights,
and the sky is like an inky black pool above my
head, I take comfort in knowing the stars are
still there, just waiting to shine through.

Marty stared down at all the little black stars
in the margin of the letter. Could this really

have been written by Vincent van Gogh? he
wondered. Or had one of Gramps's friends
found his letter under the door in the old wing
of Shady Maples and sent it on to someone in
France, who then wrote back to him? What
about the other letters? Were they real or
fake? Marty ran his fingers over the stars and
began to smile, because he suddenly realized
that it didn't matter.

Whoever had sent him the letter had made
him happy. The thought of the stars in the sky
made him smile. And the thought of Gramps
living in his heart made him smile. It was as if
he had been carrying around the big black inky
sky from *Starry Nights* in his head and now he
could see the light twinkling through.

Marty wondered if he should show the letter to his mother. He decided not to, since he
knew what she would say. She would argue,
"You can't get letters from dead people, and it
must have been written by one of Gramps's
friends." He thought about showing it to Russ,
but decided that even Russ wouldn't want to
see "another letter from a dead guy." It would
probably make him think about almost losing

his Six, and how embarrassed he had been by the whole thing. No, he wouldn't show the letter to anyone.

"It will be my secret," he whispered, looking down at all the little black stars. "Mine and maybe Henry Cooper's."

Marty raised his head at the sound of a loud creak. He jumped off his bed and ran to the window, just as the little metal box clanked against the glass. He quickly opened the window and unhooked the box.

"Hey, Measle, looks like you've got some company." He laughed as he lifted Charlie out of the box. Charlie blinked and tried to chew his finger. "Same old Charlie, still chewing." Marty grinned as he placed the mouse beside Measle in the cage. Then he went back to the box and took out the message.

Dear Avenger,

This is a BIG EMERGENCY!!! I had to send Charlie over for his own protection. If Deena finds out what he did, Charlie could be in BIG trouble. While I was getting dressed for school this morning, I let Charlie out in my room for a little exercise. I put him back in his cage, but I guess I forgot to lock it. When I came home, it was open. I looked all over and finally found him in Deena's room.

Charlie must have thought that Deena's doll house was a mouse house, because that's where I found him. He was busy chewing the legs off the tiny kitchen table! Her dollhouse doesn't look so good. Charlie chewed on the living room couch and the dining room rug. He even took a bite out of one of the dolls. If he had chewed her foot, it wouldn't be so bad, but he bit off her nose!

I'm trying to fix things as best I can with toothpicks, markers, and glue and paper. I made a little nose out of Play-Doh for the doll, and it came out pretty good, except its color (blue was the only color I had).

Deena stayed after school for band practice,

so I have to hurry up and get this all done before she comes home. Do you want to help?

Your friend,
The Flame

P.S. This is an emergency, and if you have any nose-colored Play-Doh, bring it with you.

Chapter 26

Marty rushed to Russell's house and together the two worked on repairing the dollhouse. Marty took his set of colored clay and they picked out what looked closest to a flesh color. They had such a good time making the nose that they began to make new noses for all the dolls, using a rainbow of colors. When Marty gave a pretty blond doll a long gray elephant nose, Russ laughed so hard that he fell over backward. Suddenly Marty found himself laughing too. It was the first time he had laughed since Gramps died, and it felt so good, he didn't want to stop. When he finally did, he could hear the late bus pull up to the curb outside.

Russ's eyes grew wide as they heard the bus door open. The boys quickly took the strange noses they had created off the dolls' faces. Then they raced back to Russ's room, where they broke into giggles. Pressing their ears to the bedroom door, they heard Deena running up the stairs. They stood waiting. Silence. Then footsteps and a loud cry!

"All right, who was in my room? Who gave my Cindy a green nose?" Deena screamed, running into the hall and down the stairs. Marty and Russ groaned as they realized that they must have forgotten to remove one of the noses. Russ cringed when he heard his mother's voice.

"Russell McGrath, you get down here this minute!" she yelled.

Marty and Russell didn't have to write one hundred sentences, but Russ lost television privileges for the evening.

As Marty changed into his pajamas that night, he thought about his day with Russ. Somehow things had turned around. It had been like old times, fooling around with Russ, having fun and getting into trouble. And yet, Marty knew that some things could never turn around. Gramps could never come back.

Marty glanced across the room at the little birdhouse sitting on his bookshelf. He felt a pang of sadness as he realized that he and Gramps would never get to hang it up and have that special celebration together. But then Marty smiled as he thought of all the wonderful treasures he had inside the birdhouse, and how he could always keep it with him wherever he went.

He walked to the bookcase and took the birdhouse down. He carried it to his bed and carefully began taking out the letters, one by one. He read them over. Marty suddenly understood that each letter was a gift from Gramps. Marty would never know whether or not the letters had been posted by Henry Cooper's Secret Courier Service. But his mother had been right in saying that the letters came from Gramps's love for him. And as different as they all were, each one offered Marty something he needed now. They offered him hope.

As Marty began putting the letters back in their envelopes, he realized that there was one more letter that needed to go into the birdhouse. A thank you letter. Even though he realized that it could never be mailed, Marty knew that he needed to write it, so he leaned over his bed and lifted his backpack from the floor. Then he took out his notebook and pencil.

"Marty, what are you doing still up?" his mother called from her bedroom. "Come on, lights out."

"Ten more minutes—I'm writing a letter," Marty answered.

"Oh, all right, just ten more minutes," his mother agreed. "Did you say you were writing a letter? I hope you're writing to someone who's alive this time."

"No, he's dead too," Marty whispered under his breath. "But not in my heart. Not in my heart . . ." His voice trailed off as he turned to a clean page in his notebook and began to write:

Dear Gramps, . . .